Longarm said, "Don't be calling me any of your family names, *feller*. Now turn around and walk toward that door."

The big man laughed slightly and turned his head toward the man behind him. As he did, Longarm raised his right hand as if to scratch his ear. But he only got his hand just above shoulder height. There it suddenly turned into a fist and he drove off his right foot, stepping forward with his left, putting his whole shoulder behind the punch. The blow hit the big man flush in the face just as he was turning to face Longarm again. Longarm saw his fist hit the man on the upper lip and the lower part of his nose. He saw blood fly and felt something crunch beneath his knuckles. It was either teeth or the bone in the man's nose.

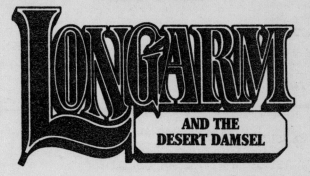

TABOR EVANS

LONGARM

AND THE DESERT DAMSEL

JOVE BOOKS, NEW YORK

LONGARM AND THE DESERT DAMSEL

A Jove Book / published by arrangement with
the author

PRINTING HISTORY
Jove edition / February 1996

The Putnam Berkley World Wide Web site address is
http://www.berkley.com

ISBN: 0-515-11807-9

A JOVE BOOK®
Jove Books are published by The Berkley Publishing Group,
200 Madison Avenue, New York, New York 10016.
JOVE and the "J" design are trademarks
belonging to Jove Publications, Inc.

PRINTED IN THE UNITED STATES OF AMERICA

10 9 8 7 6 5 4 3 2 1

Chapter 1

It had taken him two days to walk from where he'd lost his horse to the stage relay station somewhere between Gila Bend and Buckeye in the western part of the Arizona Territory. It was June and it was hot and it was the desert. He had made the walk on half a bottle of whiskey and a two-quart canteen of water. Besides that, and two cans of stewed tomatoes, he'd had nothing else to sustain him. He'd walked mostly at night, when it was cool enough to be called cold, and laid up as best he could in the featureless country during the day. There wasn't a tree or a bush or even a good rise in the ground to shelter him from the relentless sun. So there had been nothing for it except to sling his saddle over one shoulder and his saddlebags over the other and keep footing along, putting one boot in front of the other.

It hadn't been the sun so much, or his hunger and thirst. Mainly it had been his feet. He'd never willingly walked over a hundred yards in his life, and to walk as far as he was being forced to in boots had been torture. By the second day he'd developed blisters. He'd tried to toughen and cure his feet by washing them in whiskey but it hadn't done a lot of good except to make him laugh that he'd ever have used his precious, special

1

brand of Maryland whiskey to wash his feet in. But there'd been no choice. Water was too precious. He hadn't run upon many such occasions in his life when water took precedence over good whiskey, but he'd finally found one when there was no debate.

The land was rough: sandy and rocky with little patches of bunchgrass. Its only redeeming feature was that it was flat. The ground was flat and endless and the air was crystal clear and dry. He reckoned a man could see a hundred miles in any direction. In fact, he had spotted the stage relay station a full six hours before he was able to walk to it. The last of those six hours it had seemed like the little cluster of buildings and corrals was receding rather than getting closer. By the time he had staggered into the main building he was limping badly on sore and blistered feet.

His name was Custis Long and he was a deputy U.S. marshal operating out of the southwest district in Denver, Colorado. He had been a deputy marshal for longer than he cared to remember, but it was difficult to tell how old he was. His weathered and tanned face said forty years or better, but the lithe movements of his muscled, well-proportioned body said closer to thirty. He was a little over six feet tall, and even after a week in the Arizona desert still weighed about 190 pounds, because he didn't carry around much fat to lose. He was called Longarm by his friends in a good-natured way, and the same by the men he hunted and brought to law for a different reason. His last name was Long, but he was the long arm of the law because he would cross the continent to catch you if you were his quarry. Some said he would cross the ocean, but that theory had never been put to the test. But the word among the bandit community about Custis Long was that it wasn't a question of *would* he get you once he set in on your trail. The only question was how long before you found him in your pocket with your gun in his hand and his gun aimed right at you.

But as he entered the main building of the little stage

2

station his badge was in his pocket, and it would stay there unless it was needed. He didn't advertise himself as a peace officer unless he was on a job and it was necessary. He'd found that people acted differently around you when they found you were a law officer, especially a federal officer. So unless it came up for a good reason, none of the people at the stage stop would know what he did for a living.

Right at the moment he walked into the blessed shade of the way station he considered himself off duty. He had just spent a week, in cooperation with the Arizona Rangers, chasing six convicts who had escaped from the territorial prison at Yuma. They had killed and captured five of them, and Longarm had been in lone pursuit of the last one when his horse had come a cropper. If nothing else was to be gotten out of the incident, he'd learned, in a way that would never leave him, why the slender bone in the front foreleg of a horse was called the cannon bone. He had been running his horse over the flat prairie, trying to come within rifle shot of the fleeing convict, when he'd heard a sound like a gunshot. For a second, as his horse had started going down by its head and he'd made plans to try to jump clear, he'd thought his animal had been shot. But then, after he'd rolled across the sandy prairie and gotten up and dusted himself off, he'd seen his mount trying to get up. It was then he'd seen the sickening sight of the poor animal's right foreleg and the grotesque way it was bent where there was no joint. He had hastened to the animal, soothing him with one hand as he'd pulled his revolver with the other. One shot and it had been over. The animal had been just a cavalry mount he'd requisitioned at the Yuma territorial prison from the army post stationed there. Still, he hated to see any animal hurt like that. But that was the chance you took when you ran a horse hard over country that you didn't know. The western desert of Arizona was smooth to the casual eye, but it was pitted with many a hazard that could cause a horse, running at top speed, to throw himself off just enough to cause injury. Longarm had long marveled that, as big and strong as horses were, they didn't hurt themselves more considering the delicacy of their joints and some of their bones.

But after that there'd been nothing to do except to go looking for the nearest shelter. He'd had a map of the country that he'd gotten from the army, and as near as he could tell, his best hope had been to hike it for the stage station that looked on the map to be about twenty miles north of Gila Bend. He felt fortunate it was there since there was so little else in the country. Which, of course, was one of the reasons for locating the territorial prison in Yuma. As someone had once observed, Yuma was closer to Hell than to the United States. Nobody was expected to try to escape from Yuma for the simple reason that, without the resources, a man wouldn't last two days in such country. Yuma was in the extreme southwest corner of Arizona, very near an intersection with California and Mexico. You were in bad country at the prison, but it was a garden spot next to what you'd run into if you tried to flee in any direction. For that reason very few men ever successfully escaped. Oh, sometimes they got away from the prison itself, but the prison of heat and the wide-open empty spaces eventually executed them in a far more painful way than was ever used at the prison.

The breakout had been assisted. Depending on what you believed, and who you believed, either three or four men had been waiting for the six convicts when they had freed themselves from the prison. The breakout party had brought tools to free the prisoners of their leg irons, and had obviously been well provisioned. The Arizona Rangers had been called in to track the fugitives, and they in turn had called for Longarm's assistance since he had caught and imprisoned the escapees' ringleader, Carl Lowe. Longarm had taken a train down through Flagstaff, and then to Blythe, California, and then down to Yuma. By the time they'd set off in pursuit the prisoners and their accomplices had had a forty-eight-hour lead. Then there was further confusion when the Rangers had insisted that the captives would flee straight south to Mexico. Longarm had pointed out the clear sign that indicated the escapees were fleeing east, but the Rangers had been unconvinced. They'd claimed it was false sign to throw them off and further delay the pursuit. Longarm had patiently explained that the country to the immediate south was rough and uninhabited, with no water and very little in the way of fodder for the fugitives' animals. He'd taken the position that the outlaws were going to head east for some fifty or sixty miles, and then turn south into an area of Mexico that was peopled, dotted with villages, and lush with water and grass. The Rangers had resented him telling them how to operate in their territory, and Longarm had just shrugged and advised them to go their way and he'd go his. Even though he was based in Denver, much of his business was done in Arizona, New Mexico, and Texas, so he knew that country as well as he did his own back-yard. When someone had once asked him why he was always in such places he'd said, "Because that's where the outlaws are. Ain't no use hunting bandits in church, at least not the kind that carry guns."

In the end the Rangers had agreed to follow his lead, which was just as well for him since they had the pack-horses and the supplies. Four days later they'd run the crowd to ground in the Aquilla Mountains, a small range in the middle of the desert floor that the convicts and their helpers had chosen as a place to rest. In the running fight most of them had been accounted for except for three who had escaped toward the east. Longarm had followed along with the Rangers until it became clear to him that one of the men they were chasing had broken off from the others and was heading due north. There were towns in that direction and a small railroad, and Longarm had insisted the lone escapee was the most important. The Rangers had disagreed, and Longarm had taken a fresh horse, gotten him watered and fed, and then taken off in hot pursuit of the solo escapee. He had gotten close enough to see that it was a man, riding a horse and apparently pulling a pack animal. That had been when he had made the mad dash. It had come up a half a mile short. After he'd put his animal out of its misery, he'd stood for a long time staring after the small figure that was barely discernible through the shimmering heat waves. He'd felt sure it was Carl Lowe.

But there had been not a damn thing he could do about it. His first duty was to try and save government property, namely himself. He knew the Rangers wouldn't be coming to look for him, so he'd gotten out the map and begun putting sand between himself and his dead horse.

At first he thought the station was just manned by one old codger. He'd appeared almost as soon as Longarm had slumped down on a bench in the outer room. The man was thin and gaunt and had lost most of his hair, and would have lost his pants if they hadn't been held up by a frayed pair of red suspenders. But what he lacked in youth and flesh he more than made up in energy and talk. The instant he came into the room he said, "Say, been a-watchin' you a-comin' this way. Could tell right off you wasn't much of a walkin' man." He gestured at Longarm's saddle, which the marshal had dropped at his feet. "Now that thang there, case you don't know what is, that there is a outfit you put on a horse. A man ain't supposed to carry it like I seen you a-doin'. That there is a saddle and fits a horse's back." Then he cackled like he'd never had so much fun in his life.

Longarm slowly raised his head. He said, "Mister, would you have so much as a drink of water? Don't even have to be cool. Just has to be wet. I'd like to turn this sand in my throat into mud."

The quiet words seemed to have an instant effect on the man. His mouth dropped open and he said, "Why, bless Pat, whatever in this world be I a-thinkin' about." He gave his sagging trousers a quick hitch and spun on his heels. "Course you'd be wantin' water, my stars and garters! Damn fool old man! Be right back with some fresh well water."

Longarm just sat there, slumped on the bench, not feeling much of anything except the pleasant absence of the sun. He couldn't be sure because such things were hard to measure, but he might be more tired than he'd ever been in his life. Of course there had been the time some years back when he'd caught a gang of low-down scoundrels who'd robbed a whorehouse and the madam, in gratitude, had given him free run of the place for as long as he could last. He'd been pretty tired then, but he'd been younger and the young tended to bounce back faster. Right now he wasn't sure he planned to ever walk another step the rest of his life.

Then the old man was back with a wooden bucket of water and a dipper. He set it on the bench by Longarm and said, "Thar you be. Now you take some of that and then we'll see to gettin' you some other stuff might help. Don't take that water down too fast. You do and it'll cause yore stummick to dispute you."

Longarm reached for the handle of the dipper. He said, "This ain't the first time I been thirsty. Just the first time I'd rather have water than a woman. Or whiskey."

The old man, his Adam's apple bobbing up and down in his scrawny neck, said, "My stars and garters, you do be in bad shape, mister. Well, you just nurse down a little of that well water and then we'll take a measure of the sitshiation."

The water tasted of alkali and was nowhere near cool, but to Longarm it was worth about a dollar a drop. He drank a careful dipper slowly, taking a small swallow at a time but never taking the dipper from his mouth until he'd drained it. After that he put the dipper back in the pail, waited a moment, and then brought it, brimming full, back to his lips.

The old man looked alarmed. He said in his high,

7

reedy voice, "Look out! Look out! You'll founder yore-self for shore!"

But Longarm only took a short drink, and then rested the dipper on his thigh while he looked around the room he was in. The building was made of native rock and heavy timbers that appeared to Longarm to be railroad cross-ties. The room he was in was about twenty feet by twenty feet with a wooden floor and heavy timber rafters. The roof was of tin and didn't do much to cool the sun. He thought that if somebody had had the sense to put a real ceiling in the place, it might drop the temperature at least ten degrees. But it was so much cooler than outside he was not about to complain.

There were several benches like the one he was sitting on scattered about, and a long wooden table with backless benches. He figured that was the dining table. There was also a big fireplace at one end, and a plank set across two barrels with some bottles of whiskey behind it. That, Longarm guessed, was the bar, though what a bar was doing in such a place was beyond his ability to comprehend, at least for the moment.

He could see that there was another room in the back, and then an entrance to a breezeway that ran to another building that was smaller than the one he was in. He reckoned the building at the end of the short breezeway was the cookshack or kitchen. It was a common practice in such country to set the kitchen off from the rest of the house. The poor cook might roast, but there was no sense in the rest of the house having to suffer from the extra heat. The other room, he guessed, must be the private quarters of the stationkeeper, who he assumed was the old man. He guessed he was in a kind of passenger room, though what such an extravagance was doing in a relay station was more than he could imagine. On any stage line in the Southwest and West relay stations were set up approximately every twenty miles, depending on the terrain. That was the distance a team could be expected to make good speed. A relay station, therefore, existed solely for the purpose of hooking on a fresh team

8

and giving rest and sustenance to the animals that had just come off their run. But sometimes such places were designated as holdover stops for the passengers so they could have a meal and a rest from the arduous travel. Those places were usually where the change of driver and shotgun guard occurred. Without moving his head much Longarm guessed that this relay station was one of those places.

The water was starting to revive him, but it was also letting him know just how nearly done in he'd come close to being. Longarm took another drink and then said in a croaky voice, "I got to get these boots off. Feet are in a hell of a shape."

The old man went to bend over, but Longarm stopped him. "No, they can't be pulled off, not just like that." He put the dipper down, leaned over, and pulled up his jeans until the tops of his boots were exposed. "Pour some water in there, if you will," he said.

The old man picked up the bucket, but before he poured he said, "Blisters?"

Longarm nodded. "On blisters."

"Hot damn!" the old man said. "You be in luck, mister. My old woman is out back bilin' clothes right now in lye soap. She gets finished, I'll fetch in some of that lye water. Best thang in the world for galled feet!"

Longarm said tiredly, "Let's get the boots off before we go to soaking my feet."

He watched while the old man poured a generous amount of water down the top of each boot. Even though it was nearly lukewarm, the water brought instant relief to his aching, burning feet. Fortunately he'd been wearing an old pair of boots that that had nearly put in their time and were worn and loose. But still, his feet were so swollen he knew it was going to be a chore to get the boots off. But the water would make the leather slicker and cause it to expand just a little.

The old man said, "You ready to give 'er a try?"

Longarm looked at the wooden floor. It was scarred

and stained, but it was still inside the house. He said, "I reckon we better go outside. I dump a load of water on your wife's floor, she's liable to run me back out in that desert."

But the old man said, "Pshaw! She don't kere a fig 'bout that. This ol' floor has seen worse than a little water on it." He bent down and took hold of Longarm's right boot. "Let 'er rip."

Longarm leaned back and slowly wiggled and pulled. Slowly his stockinged foot emerged. It had come out much easier than he'd thought, and not so much water had spilled on the floor.

"Now the other'n. I'll take 'er right easy an' you sing out iffen I'm goin' too quick."

In another moment he was sitting in his stocking feet, his head down almost between his knees. The left foot appeared more swollen. At least it had wanted out of the boot less than the right. Longarm took a long slow breath while the old man took his boots outside to empty the rest of the water out of them. He was about to call out for the stationkeeper not to leave his boots in the sun to dry when the old man appeared with them and put them carefully against the wall, saying, "I'll grease the inside of these with some tallow I got. Keep 'em from stiffening up. You better get them stockings off and let's see what we got to work with."

Slowly, painfully, Longarm peeled off his thick, woolen socks and then looked down at his feet. They were dead white except for some angry blothes along the sides and the back. There were red spots on a few of his toes and the balls of each feet, but they looked considerably better than he'd expected.

The old man said, "Why, pshaw, them ain't so bad. I seen worse on horses had to be shot."

Longarm said, mumbling, "I washed 'em in whiskey."

The old man's head shot up. Longarm could see the

signs of a drinker in his eyes and his face. "You warshed 'em in *what*?"

"Whiskey. I started out I had two quarts of water and a half a quart of whiskey." With an effort he unslung the strap of the canteen from around his neck. It clanked to the floor with an empty sound. "I got here with no water, but a little bonded Maryland corn whiskey. I think the alcohol saved my feet."

The old man looked at him, marveling. He said, "I heard me many a trick in my time, but that is the beatenist. Takes some kind of man to give the whiskey to his feet and the water to his belly. My stars and garters, you'll be up and around in no time. How far you say you walked?"

Longarm shook his head. "Don't know. Walked for two days. Never done that before. How far can a man walk in two days? Ten miles? Twenty?"

"More like thirty or forty if he stays at it right steady. Say you got lost?"

Longarm half smiled. "Something like that. Horse broke his leg."

The old man stood up and frowned. "You ain't tellin' me you was out in yonder country with just the one mount?"

Longarm took off his hat and wipped his brow. He set his hat along the bench to let his head cool off if it would and said, "Well, I hadn't planned it that way, but that's the way it worked out. You the stationkeeper?"

"Yessir, yessir," the old man said. He put out a bony hand. "Higgins be the name. Herman Higgins. Right glad to see you."

Longarm shook hands. "Name is Custis Long, Mr. Higgins. I am right grateful for your help. I had me a map and this looked to be the closest help. I'm glad you were here."

The old man's face went blank "Wa'l, I'll be straight with you, mister," he said, "they was just about a fuzz away from skiddin' the whole kit and caboodle twenty miles west, but I talked 'em out of it right at the last minute. I said, reckon what would happen if some pilgrim come walkin' in from the east an' we was gone! Wouldn't want that on yore conscious, would you? Well, sir, they seen my point and they took it an' that's why you found us where we be.''

Longarm tried to smile, but he couldn't put much into it. He said, ''Well, anyway, my feet thank you.''

The old man snapped his fingers as if he had just recollected something important. ''The lye water!'' He scooped up the bucket by the rope handle and took off toward the back. ''Won't be ary a minute!''

''Not too hot!'' Longarm yelled after him. ''And not too strong!''

He wasn't all that sold on lye water. From what little he'd heard about people getting blisters on their feet, you were supposed to grease them down good with axle grease or some such. Lye water seemed a trifle harsh a treatment.

But even then, with his feet paining him and his body given out and used up and dried out, he was still rankled about Carl Lowe. The man now had a minimum of two days on him, but as soon as Longarm could lay his hands on a horse he intended to be right back after Lowe. He had a pretty good idea where Lowe was going, and if he could arrive in time, he thought he might catch up with the man.

Higgins came bustling back with his bucket. It was full of grayish water that smelled a little like sulphur and had steam rising from it. Longarm calculated that any liquid that had steam rising from it in the heat of an Arizona day was hotter than he cared to stick anything in, especially his sore feet. He said, ''Water that down a little, Mr. Higgins, if you please. And cool it off.''

Higgins said happily, ''Oh, it'll be just fine in a minute. You just set right still while I fetch you a restorative.''

Longarm watched while the wiry little man sprang across the room, went behind his makeshift bar, and

12

poured something out of a bottle into a glass. At first Longarm had thought Higgins was along in his sixties, but he had so much energy and verve that Longarm was rapidly revising his estimate downward. Higgins looked no bigger than a scrawny banty rooster, and his crop of three-or four-day-old whiskers was peppered with white, but he had the energy of a man not much more than forty or so. He came bounding back to Longarm holding out a water glass half full of an amber liquid. He said proudly, "That there is rum. And it is rum of the finest kind. That is Spanish rum made down in Mexico. I generally charge four bits a shot for that drink, but it is on the house seeing as how I am rescuing you."

Longarm took the glass doubtfully. Given a choice of drinking the lye water or the rum, it might have been a tossup. He drank whiskey by choice, and would drink brandy or wine or beer, but he had never cared for rum. But he couldn't hurt the old man's feelings. And besides, it might make him feel better. He put the glass to his lips and drank off half the liquor, repressing a shudder. If Higgins thought what he had was *good* rum, then Longarm didn't want to try any he was not so proud of.

But he said, "Aaaaah. Boy, that hit the spot."

Higgins nudged the bucket close to Longarm's feet. " 'Bout time we got on with the doctorin'."

Longarm looked at the water and then at his tender-looking feet. He picked them up and held them poised over the bucket. Then slowly and tentatively, he gradually eased them down in the murky waters. At first he thought the water was too hot, but then he realized it was the lye water playing hell with the raw places on his feet. He let out a yowl and jerked his feet out of the bucket. Glaring at Higgins, he said, "Damn, Herman, that kind of smarts! How about weakening that down a little?"

Higgins looked doubtful, but he went over to the long, rough dining table and came back with a pitcher of water. With Longarm urging him on, he finally poured about a glassful of fresh water in the bucket. He said, "Ain't gonna do you no good a'tall iffen it ain't got some bite to it."

Longarm gave him a look and growled that it had more bite than a bulldog as it was. Then he grudgingly put his feet back in the water. The dilution, as far as he was concerned, had not helped a bit. But he gritted his teeth and forced himself to keep his feet down in the bucket. Such was the agony that he even emptied the glass of rum without tasting it.

Higgins said, "See, what it does is toughens up the skin so it ain't raw and sore anymore."

Longarm said, "I believe if a man was to bathe in the stuff, it would toughen his hide so he'd come out bulletproof. If it didn't kill him."

Higgins said, "Let me get you another restorative." And before Longarm could stop him he'd plucked the glass out of his hand and skipped over to the bar to fetch back some more of his "fine Spanish rum."

Longarm said, "You ain't got so much as a cigar around here, do you? Or a rope that is smokable?"

"Got a seegar!" Higgins said triumphantly. "Got two of 'em, as a matter of fact. Might have a little age on 'em. We ain't exactly set up for retail trade."

Higgins brought the drink back and handed it, along with a musty-looking cigar, to Longarm. Then he found himself a ladder-backed cane-bottomed chair and drew it up in front of the marshal. He said, "Walked two days, did ya. I reckon you are glad to set a spell."

Longarm found a match and got the cigar drawing, though it was hard work. He took a sip of the rum, to be polite, and said, "Mr. Higgins, I've got to get my hands on a horse. I got business up the road."

Higgins shook his head. "I'm mighty sorry to tell you that you are out of luck in that department. And the southbound stage done come through this morning, and the northbound ain't due for three days."

Longarm drew hard at the cigar. It was at least tobacco. "It's north I need to go, Mr. Higgins. Surely you've got some kind of horse around here. Hell, this is a relay station.''

Higgins nodded. He swept his arm toward the back of the room. "You walk right out there, mister, an' you can pick you out any Spanish mule you want. Probably got thirty on the place. You want to travel up the road on one of them little onery cusses, you are more than welcome.''

Longarm grimaced. He was irritated at himself. He knew this stage line. Knew its route and knew its purpose. It ran from the gold mines down near the Mexican border beginning at Lukeville up through Gunsight, to Ajo, through Gila Bend, and finally into Buckeye, where it linked up with the railroad that ran east and west out of Phoenix. It was not really a passenger line, its main purpose being the hauling of gold bullion out of the mines located around the Organ Pipe Cactus Mountains. They didn't even use the big, comfortable Butterfield coaches, preferring wagons that were about twice the size of a buckboard and were covered with a canvas top. They were pulled by a team of eight fine-boned Spanish mules that could go at a gallop for the twenty miles between relay stations, and then maybe go another twenty before they dropped dead. The teams were so hard to stop that, sometimes, the driver had to circle his team out in front of the station until the stationkeeper, or someone, could get hold of the leaders and bring them to a halt. No horses were ever used in the rough and dry country. They couldn't take it the way the little mules could. Unfortunately, the little mules were too ornery to make riding stock.

Longarm said, "Damn!" He thought a minute. "Mr. Higgins, I've got important business to the north that just won't wait three days. Ain't you got some kind of wagon or buggy I could hitch a couple of those mules to?" He reached into his pocket and partially exposed his roll of bills. "If it is a matter of money . . .''

Higgins looked sad. "Mr. Long, I'd mighty like to accommodate you and without a dollar bein' spent. But the fact is these here mules an' all the property, fer that matter, is company property an' ain't mine to do with as I sees fit. So money don't come into it at all. I taken a likin' to you right from the start. Man gone through what you'd done an' still had him a sense of humor. So I'd he'p you if I could. But the fact of the business is that they ain't a conveyance or a buggy or even a sled that will get you a mile from this place. Now, I don't know if that thinkin' is directed at the stationkeeper or not, but they won't let me nor none of the rest keep a horse or anything else a body can use for travel. The stationkeeper arrives here on the stage, an' when he is ready to quit the place he's got to leave on the stage." Higgins snorted. "Make a man think them folks didn't trust us to stay on the job."

Longarm suppressed a smile. "Well, it would seem that way," he said. He slowly stood, his feet still in the lye water, and looked down at himself. "Lord, I'm a mess. I'd give a pretty penny to get washed off."

Higgins said, "You got clean clothes?"

Longarm nodded toward his saddlebags. "Oh, yes. But I ain't putting them on as filthy as I am."

Higgins began bobbing his head. "You just never mind that. You soak yore feet a little time more, an' I'll go out back and run my ol' woman in the house, and you can take this bucket out by the well and just douse yourself down. How's that sound?"

Longarm said, "Sounds mighty good to me. What about the grub department? I ain't had much in that line the last three or four days."

Higgins's head bobbed again. "You never mind that. We'll get that tended to in time. Now, whyn't you go ahead and set down and finish yore rum, an' I'll go out an' tell the old woman to get set to move her matters into the house." He gestured at Longarm's clothes.

16

"An' she can give them a washing whilst she is about it."

Longarm sat back down on the bench and watched as Higgins hurried out the back. He was the busiest person Longarm thought he'd ever seen. When the stationkeeper was out of sight, Longarm thoughtfully poured the rest of his glass of rum down in the lye water. He figured it would do his feet a hell of a lot more good than it would his stomach.

But Higgins was also wrong about the mules and the other company property. They weren't his to lend or give, but they were Longarm's to requisition. The stage line was a public conveyance running over a public road with the government's permission. Longarm, as a federal officer, could make use of anything he chose, from a mule to a coach and driver if it came down to it. But right then, he didn't want Higgins to know he was a federal marshal. The old man was already falling all over himself with hospitality. Longarm couldn't imagine what he'd be like if he caught sight of the badge. Just then Higgins came in from the back. "Mr. Long, we be gettin' all set up for you out back. My ol' woman is gatherin' up her doin's and the back will be yor'n. 'Less you be over-modest, you ought to be able to get yoreself a good cleanin' up. I reckon I can maybe even find you somethin' to dry off with."

Longarm said, "I doubt that will be necessary, Mr. Higgins. I reckon the hard part will be to get any water to stay on without drying up in that sun before a man can do any washing."

He stepped carefully out of the bucket of lye water. He'd expected his feet to be very tender on the rough wood floor, but they felt surprisingly normal. He looked down. They were as white as ever, but a good deal of the redness had gone. He said, surprised, "Hell, Mr. Higgins, I think this lye water might have been just the ticket."

The old man nodded vigorously. "Do it ever' time. That there stuff will cure ever'thang from a hernia to a broken heart. You get yore gear and I'll fetch that bucket. You can use it to douse down with.''

Longarm gathered up his saddlebags and limped across the floor. But he was limping more in fear of pain than actual pain.

Higgins said, ''Soon's we get you stripped, I'll give yore dirty duds to the ol' woman an' she'll get 'em slicked up nice an' clean for you.''

It was coming on to late afternoon. Longarm and Higgins were sitting where they had previously. Longarm was wearing a pair of clean, heavy wool socks. He was not about to try his boots yet, and in fact, Higgins had discouraged the idea vigorously until Longarm's feet had had two or three more treatments of the lye water. Longarm was feeling almost human. He was clean and wearing clean clothes and had managed to shave, though working up a lather with lye soap produced about the same results as if he had been using a rock. The only thing missing for his return to normal was food. He spoke to Higgins about it, making sure Higgins understood he could pay.

Higgins said, ''Now, we do be a vittles station fer the passengers. They lays over here right at a half to three quarters of an hour, depending on what a rush the driver is in. They gets the company fare of pinto beans and grits and cornmeal and either canned tomatoes or canned peaches. We give 'em coffee too. Course we ain't got no beef. But ever' dern fool comes through here expects a steak and will even demand it.'' He shook his head and snorted. ''A few months in the winter and we can nurse a side of beef along, but right now? Hell.'' He pointed toward the front of the building. ''Was I to hang a side of beef out there at sundown, it'd be froze nearly by dawn. Then, by mid-mornin' it'd be plumb thawed. By noon you'd be walkin' upwind of it, and by three in the afternoon a fly wouldn't light on it.'' He gave a disgusted sound. ''An' there is them as comes in here wantin' beef! My stars and garters.''

Longarm said, "Some of them beans and grits and cornbread sound pretty good to me."

Higgins threw up his head. "Why, nosir! Not on yore tintype! Why, I feel like I brung you back from the dead. Me and my ol' woman keep ham and bacon fer ourselves, and she's got her a run full of chickens out there. Fries one up on occasion or makes dumplin's with it. My ol' woman kin cook, I'm a-tellin' you."

Longarm had met Higgins's "ol' woman." She had proved to be a pleasant-faced woman in her late thirties or early forties. What flesh Higgins was missing she had taken for herself. Not that she was fat, Longarm thought, just pleasantly plump. He wondered how she stayed so good-natured out in the middle of the desert.

Longarm said, "I wouldn't want to put her to no trouble. Sylvia." That was her first name, and she had insisted that Longarm call her that.

"Pshaw!" Higgins exclaimed. "She'd get her feelin's hurt she would if you didn't let her cook fer you. I'll get her to whomp you up a big bait of eggs and biscuits, and would you druther ham or bacon?"

"Ham's fine with me. And I would sure drink a cup of coffee. Still got a little of my whiskey left to sweeten it with."

Higgins got up to go deliver Longarm's order. He frowned. "Now you don't be shy 'bout drinkin' my rum. Ain't no use in swillin' down them corn squeezin's when they is good rum to drink."

Longarm tried to look guileless. Privately he was about halfway convinced that it was the half-glass of rum he'd poured in the lye water that had done his feet the most good, but he didn't want to take the slightest chance on hurting his host's feelings. "Herman," he said, "I am much obliged, and I know a good drink when I taste one. But I got to tell you, that little trip through the desert left me in a kind of weakened state and I ain't up to that stout a drink just yet. I reckon I better stick to corn whiskey."

Higgins snapped his fingers. "My stars and garters! I

19

never thought! What in the world is the matter with me." He shook his head and slapped himself on the forehead. "I'm gettin' the poorest set of manners in the country. Sylvie will be on me I don't watch out. And oh, can she be a wampus kitty! Whoooeee!"

When Higgins came back, Longarm was trying to smoke the second cigar the old man had given him. But when he'd bathed and shaved he'd managed to clean his teeth with some baking soda and salt, and his clean mouth only showed off the age of the cigar more. Nevertheless, he was giving it a valiant effort. He'd had a good swallow of his Maryland whiskey, and was feeling content except for the worrisome problem of Carl Lowe.

He said to Higgins, "Herman, I have just got to get up north. I need to make it to a railroad junction somewhere close to Phoenix. Are you and your wife the only ones here?"

"Well, they is the two Mexicans helps me with the stock. But they ain't got nothin'. I tell you, Mr. Long, the company jes' won't let you have no way to get around on yore own. They done lost too many station-keepers like that. Gets mighty lonesome and mean out c'here and some folks can't take it and they light 'em a shuck out of the place. Been plenty drivers come pulling in to a station with a team all lathered up and snorty and nobody to meet 'em and no fresh team ready. Course I tell 'em if they'd get married couples like me an' the ol' woman, they wouldn't have that trouble."

"Yeah," Longarm said, discouraged. "I can see how that would be a problem for them." He grimaced. "That next station north is twenty miles, right?"

"Yessir."

He studied the far wall for a moment. "I wonder if I could ride one of those little mules twenty miles. I wonder who'd give out first, him or me."

Higgins said, "I doubt if it could be managed. I got to tell you, Mr. Long, them mules ain't the tamest critters you ever been around. And they damn shore ain't saddle-broke, as them Mexicans has found out to their sorrow. You must have some all-fired powerful business waitin' on you to have you frettin' like this. Laws, it ain't been much more'n five hours since you staggered in here near dead. Now you are afire to get on out under that sun again.''

Longarm sat thinking for a moment. Maybe he was worrying himself overmuch and maybe for nothing. For all he knew the man that had gotten away had not been Carl Lowe. Maybe Carl Lowe was either dead or back in prison, and some two-bit outlaw had disappeared over the horizon leaving Longarm staring after him. But Longarm couldn't help worrying. He worried because Carl Lowe was a man to worry about. Not that he was a violent man or a gunhand or even a murderer. His history showed that he had never raised a hand against his fellow man in anger in all his life. Nevertheless, he was as dangerous a man to the economic well-being of the Southwest territories as there was around.

For most of his life Carl Lowe had been a quiet, law-abiding citizen who had worked for the Wells Fargo Company in California in its original business of transporting gold bullion from mine sites to government mints. Carl Lowe was a man of well-above-average intelligence and was of a mechanical bent. He had devised some of the first safes and strongboxes that Wells Fargo had used. In time he had become their chief designer of methods for getting gold and silver safely from one place to another. And along the way he had become something of an expert locksmith.

Then he had suddenly disappeared and, not long afterward, there had come reports from survivors of train robberies that there was a man who could take a few tools and open a safe it would have taken twenty sticks of dynamite to blow open. And do it pretty quick in the process. It wasn't just Wells Fargo safes either. The brand or manufacturer didn't seem to matter. This quiet little man who went to work while the rest of the gang stood around with drawn revolvers could open anything. That was a valuable man to have around. Blowing up safes was a risky business. Most robbers didn't know much about dynamite, and they generally ended up blowing themselves and the safe and whatever money or gold there was all across the landscape.

It had taken two years of hard work, but Longarm had finally run Carl Lowe to ground. What had made him so hard to catch was that he would not attach himself to any one gang. He was a freelance and rented out his services to whoever could afford him. Then, once the job was finished, he would simply take his proceeds and disappear. After a long, frustrating search Longarm had finally run him to ground by employing the services of a sentenced bank robber who would get a reduced term in prison if he could put Longarm in touch with the elusive Mister Lowe. It had worked. Representing himself as a man who intended to rob a train, Longarm had finally met Carl Lowe. In the course of their conversation Lowe, to make clear his value, had recited the details of his last few jobs. It had been the same as a confession and Longarm had arrested him immediately. Lowe had drawn twenty-five years in prison, but had not even served one when the prison break had occurred.

Longarm was convinced that the breakout had been arranged for only one man, Carl Lowe, and that the other convicts who'd been freed had been used to scatter and confuse the pursuit. That part, Longarm thought grimly, had worked. He'd tried to make it clear to the Arizona Rangers what the prison break was all about, but they hadn't been willing to listen. To them, one escaped convict was the same as another. When Longarm had tried to tell them that the whole affair had been arranged by some gang needing Carl Lowe's services, they'd looked at him like he'd fallen on his head.

But still, he did not know for sure that Carl Lowe was

22

still on the loose. He might be dead and buried by now. He said to Higgins, "I take it there's just you and Sylvia and the two Mexicans here?"

Higgins scratched his balding head. "Wa'l, thar's the doctor and the hoor. Though truth be told, I ain't all that shore he be a doctor. Stays drunk mostly. He got off the soutbound stage with the hoor."

Longarm blinked. He said, "The what?"

"The doctor?"

"No, the other."

"The hoor?"

Chapter 2

Longarm frowned, perplexed. "What in hell is a 'hoor'?"

Higgins pulled his head back. "Why, you look long enough in the tooth you'd of run across a few hoors in yore time. I ain't never had no truck with 'em myself, me an' Missus Higgins bein' married long's we have. But they do a right good trade amongst the single men and them as ain't around no girls."

Longarm blinked for a minute. "Are you talking about a whore?"

"Ain't that what I been sayin'? One of them women the ladies of the church is always tryin' to get run out of town. One of them you pays."

"A whore, a prostitute."

Higgins gave him a matter-of-fact look. "Wa'l, you can dress it up in all kinds of highfalutin words if you be of a mind, but a hoor is a hoor and that is that." He put up a hand. "Now, don't get me wrong. I ain't got nothin' agin 'em personal. I be of the live-and-let-live school. Poor girl probably got led astray somehow. This one is a mighty pitiful case. Got throwed out by her own kind. Just this mornin'. She was on the southbound coach. Was a whole gaggle of 'em goin' down to Gunsight to work the miners that work in the gold mines down there. I reckon them girls make more money than the miners, you take my meaning. Their lode don't ever run out.''

''And she's here?''

Higgins waved vaguely at the door that led off the big room. ''She be back there in our private quarters takin' a rest. Missus Higgins felt right sorry for the little thang. I reckon she got some rough treatment.''

''What happened?''

Higgins shook his head. ''Durned if I know. Coach pulled in with that doctor, if he is, which I doubt, and a passel of them hoors. Was five of 'em. They was all yellin' and screamin' at this young woman that be back in the bedroom. Wouldn't let her go on with them. Seemed they was some kind of company and they fired her right here. Turns out she is in a kind of fix. Ain't got a nickel to her name and no return ticket back north.'' He shook his head. ''I reckon we'll have to try and help her some.''

''What did she do? I mean, to get the other ladies, hoors, mad at her? Was they cussing her?''

Higgins shrugged. ''I never took in the whole of it. That doctor come staggerin' up first and claimed he was sick and needed him a drink of whiskey right pronto or he was gonna cave in. I was behind the bar fixin' him up when this young woman, Rita her name is, come through kind of lookin' down in the mouth and tryin' not to cry. Was Missus Higgins kind of took her in hand. Then the doctor, if he is one, passed out on me, and I couldn't get the driver and his guard to help me load him back aboard the stage, it just bein' a quick stop, and they went on. Them other'ns was a bunch of painted women if you ever seen any. Whooooee!''

Longarm was about to ask another question about the doctor and his wherabouts when Mrs. Higgins came in with his meal. She'd fried him half a dozen eggs and given him a good big ham steak, along with grits and ham gravy and biscuits and honey. On her second trip she brought him a pot of coffee and put a cup in front of him and one in front of Mister Higgins. For the next half hour Longarm didn't do much talking or thinking, just concentrated on reducing the pile of groceries in front of him to a bare plate. But one thought that occurred to him as he ate was the telegraph wire. Most stage lines had one, and he'd seen the line as he'd staggered up to the station. He knew it would be a private line and was only strung from one end of the stage run to the other. But it was a method of communicating. He could have Higgins wire to the operator in Buckeye and have *him* wire, through the public telegraph, to Yuma to find out who had been caught and who had gotten away. It would mean revealing to Higgins that he was a deputy marshal, but he reckoned the old man would keep it to himself.

Higgins had brought him a bottle of whiskey and he'd sweetened up his coffee with it. It was nowhere near as good as his Maryland whiskey, but then he didn't have much of that left, and there was no use wishing for steak when all you had to eat was suet.

His mind turned for a second to the "hoor," Rita, and the doctor. He wondered where the doctor was, and for just a moment his mind played with the idea that the man might be Carl Lowe. But that didn't make any sense. Still, he wanted a look at him and he wanted a look at the girl. Finally he pushed his plate back, unable to eat another bite. He said, "Whew! Herman, your missus can cook up a storm! Lord, I ain't tasted anything that good since I don't know when." He ran a critical eye over Higgins. "Herman, what I can't understand is how come you don't run to more flesh the way Sylvia feeds."

Higgins shrugged. "Beats me and the missus both. Ain't got ary a idea. Oh, it ain't 'cause I don't eat. I can pack it away with the best of 'em. Sylvie says it's because I never sit still long enough for any of it to stick."

Longarm smiled. "Yeah, you do kind of remind me of a chapparal the way you dart around, busy as a bee.

26

You are of kind of a nervous nature.''

"Sylvie says I wear my clothes out from the inside the way I fidget around in 'em."

Longarm said, "Herman, I reckon you got an instrument where you can tap into that telegraph line running outside."

"Aw, yeah," Higgins said. "Got a wire runs right here into the house. Got me a key back yonder in the livin' quarters." He gave Longarm a serious eye. "Company won't hire you till you learn to tap out that code with that key. Took me a spell to get it down, but I'm a pretty fair hand now. Course ain't much call to ever use it. Ask for supplies to be sent. One thing and another. Notify other stations when a stage is runnin' way late or when we have a breakdown."

Longarm said, "Well, that is right handy, Herman, because I'm going to need you to send a message for me."

Higgins frowned, and then he looked sorrowful. He scratched behind his ear. He said, "Doggone it, Mr. Long, ain't nothin' I'd like better'n to accommodate you but, see, this here telegraph line ain't public. It be a private operation for the company I work for. They don't allow no private use if you take my meaning."

Longarm said, "I'm going to need you to make an exception for me, Herman. It's pretty important."

Higgins was looking very uncomfortable. "Now, Mr. Long, I done took a likin' to you an' I'd shore like to help. But it'd be worth my job I was to get on that instrument and be sendin' out messages hadn't got nothin' to do with company business. I'd give anything if I could, but I can't."

Longarm said, "Herman, I'm going to show you something and I'm going to depend on you being able to keep a secret. Can you do that? I got reasons for it."

Higgins pulled his head back and gave Longarm a look that said the question should never have been asked. "Pshaw!" he said. "Why, Mr. Long, they is secrets been dropped in me six, seven years ago and ain't

27

hit bottom yet. That is how deep my secret poke is. Why, my stars and bars, if it is a secret you want kept, then I am yore man."

Longarm said, "Just be sure you keep that in mind." He reached into his shirt pocket and pulled out his badge. He laid it on the table. "Herman, I'm a deputy United States marshal and I need to use your telegraph wire on official business. And since you are a transportation outfit that is regulated by the federal government, you are obliged to aid me in any way you can."

Higgins stared at the badge with his mouth open. "My stars and bars and Gertie's girdle! Take a look at that thar! Hot damn, I knowed you was somebody special minute you come staggerin' in off that desert. Somethin' told me to treat this feller right because he is a he-horse! An' by golly, I was right! Wait'll I tell the missus!"

Longarm wagged a finger at him. "No, no. This is between me and you."

Higgins's face fell. "You mean to say I got me a real live federal marshal here an' I can't even tell my ol' woman? Glory be! You have any idea how wearin' this place is on a body? Biggest excitement we get is a sand-storm, an' here you come an' I can't even say nothin'. Pshaw!"

"Herman, this is important government business. It might be that it doesn't matter who knows, but right now I'm kind of operating in the dark, so I think it's best just to play my cards pretty close to my shirt buttons. You take my meaning?"

Higgins's eyes got round. "Boy, howdy, yessir, I do, Mis—Marshal Long. I . . ." He suddenly stopped and stared at Longarm. "Yore last name be Long, don't it?"

"Yes. So what?"

Higgins said slowly, "They is a right famous federal marshal got the nickname of Longarm. Now that wouldn't be you, would it?"

Longarm shrugged. "I get called that from time to time."

Higgins let out a long breath. "Laws a-mercy! Dog

my cats if that don't beat all. I got the very marshal they call Longarm settin' right here at my table! Man that has caught more outlaws than the whole of the Texas and Arizona Rangers put together! You talk about your red-letter days! Whooooeeee!''

Longarm smiled slightly. "Herman, you are going to have to collect yourself here. Now where is your telegraph set up?''

Higgins jerked his head toward a door. "Back there in our livin' quarters. I bet what you are gonna send is gonna be real secret, ain't it?''

Longarm frowned. "Well, I'm seeking information. It ain't all that secret.''

"Boy, I'd give a dollar to know what it was all about.''

Longarm stared at him in disbelief. "But Herman, you will know. You are the one going to send and receive for me. I don't know how to work one of those damn things.''

Higgins's eyes got big again. "Great sakes alive! That's right. I'm gonna be in the know. Hot damn!''

Longarm looked at the door to the living quarters. "You said that girl was back there?''

"Yeah, she be layin' on the bed. Or she was.''

"Well, I'd rather not have anybody back there who isn't necessary. Which means just you and me. Like I say, this may come to nothing, but I'd still rather keep it mum.''

Higgins began moving around vigorously inside his clothes. He got an earnest look on his face. "Wa'l, you can count on me, Marshal Long, Longarm.'' He shook his head. "Damn, I can't believe you are settin' under my very roof. Why, you are more famous than Billy the Kid or William Cody or any of 'em. My dogs and cats!''

"I need to do this pretty quick," Longarm said. But in the back of his mind he was wishing that his boss, Chief Marshall Billy Vail, could hear what Higgins had said.

Higgins immediately leapt to his feet. "Right you are,

Cap'n. You just step this way."

Longarm followed him through an open door and into a small sitting room. It was rough and small, but Longarm could easily see the touches Sylvia had added to make the place more livable. Over in the corner Longarm saw a little table and, sitting on it, a telegraph key. A wire ran in through the small window to make the connection to the line running outside.

Higgins had gone to the door of another room and Longarm followed him, looking over his shoulder. Inside there was a woman lying on the bed. At first she appeared quite plain and a good ways past her youth. But she jumped to her feet as soon as Higgins opened his mouth, and stood beside the bed smoothing her skirt. Then he could see that she was no more than twenty-five or twenty-six and quite appealing. She wasn't beautiful, but she had a buxom figure and a pretty enough face. There was something hard in her eyes and in the set of her mouth, but Longarm thought that was just brought on by her recent hard luck.

Higgins said, "Miss Rita, I hate to disturb you but me and this gentleman got business back here. If you could wait out yonder in the common room I'd be much obliged. There is that padded bench if you are still a little light-headed."

"No," she said, "I'm fine. Tell your wife how much I appreciate her kindness."

Longarm liked her voice. It was soft and controlled and sounded as if the woman had been around people of quality. He said, "Sorry to disturb you."

She ran a cool, appraising look over him as she walked past. "Don't concern yourself," she said. "I was ready to get up."

They waited until she was through the door and in the public room, and then Higgins went to the door of their private quarters and closed it. It was a good, heavy door, and Longarm felt they couldn't be overheard. He said, "Mr. Higgins, if you'll take your place at the key, I'll tell you what to say."

As if he was about to perform some sort of ceremony, Higgins went solemnly to the little table and sat down, adjusting his chair just so. Over his shoulder he said. "I got to get on line an' give the man at the other end my signature. First thang you got to do. It's by the book."

"You do that."

With a certain awkwardness Higgins tapped out a few words with the key. Longarm didn't know what he had said because he didn't know Morse code. He'd always been intending to learn, but had somehow never gotten around to it. Higgins sat back in his chair and waited. He explained over his shoulder to Longarm, "Now I got to wait for the other end. That's the feller on duty in Buckeye."

Longarm nodded. "Sounds mighty complicated to me, Herman. I'd never be able to do this without your help."

Higgins preened. "Always happy to help the law. And especially law like you, Marshal Long. How well does a feller have to get to know you to call you Longarm?"

Longarm suppressed a smile. "Actually, I ain't all that fond of the name. Most of my friends call me Custis. I reckon we know each other good enough for that, Herman."

Just then the key started chattering. Higgins listened until it fell silent, then looked around at Longarm. "He be ready for us. You can let 'er rip."

"You don't need me to write it down?"

"Naw. Jes' give it to me in fits and starts. I'll get it."

Longarm said, "Something I forgot to mention. The man at the other end has got to be able to get to a main telegraph line. Hook into it or something. This telegram is going to the warden at Yuma prison."

Higgins's mouth fell open, but he recovered. "Oh, that ain't shakes fer him to do. He's right there on the railroad at Buckeye and he's already hooked into that regular telegraph line, whatever you call it. The one runs alongside railroads."

31

"All right. Then you need to tell him to wire the warden at Yuma and ask him what happened to the escaped prisoners from the breakout a week ago. This is official business and I need to know in a hurry. Be sure and make it clear that it is Deputy U.S. Marshal Custis Long inquiring. I need to know about all the prisoners. Make that part plain. Now, have you got that?"

"Plain as paint." Higgins hunched over his key and slowly began tapping out his message. As he worked he said, "I reckon that ol' boy on the other end is gettin' the September surprised outten him that this is comin' from a shore-'nough federal marshal. I reckon he'll burn that line up to Yuma."

He tapped for a few more minutes and then stopped and sat back. "We'll see if he got it."

In a moment the key chattered for a few seconds and then fell silent. Higgins looked over his shoulder at Longarm. "Charley, that's the feller at the other end, wants to know if I know a man can get fired pranking around on the company telegraph."

Longarm stepped forward. "You tell Charley that it is a federal offense to interfere with a United States marshal in the performance of his duty and that Marshal Custis Long is not taking kindly to this delay. Understand?"

"I reckon I do." Higgins put his finger to the key and sent the message in short, staccato bursts. When he finished he looked pleased. "I reckon that will build a fire under him," he said.

The key chattered, but only for a second. Higgins said, "That got his attention, but he says it will be a few minutes as the main line south is tied up. I'll need to set right here. Whyn't you go get you a drink of whiskey."

"I think I will," Longarm said.

"I got to stay here close."

"All right." Longarm opened the door and walked out into the public room. He went over to the bar, found a likely-looking bottle, and poured himself a drink. The young woman was sitting at the bench near the front door where his saddle still lay. He said without looking at her, "Care for a drink?"

"No, thank you."

"I'm buying."

She hesitated. "I . . . No, thank you."

But he poured her a drink anyway, crossed the common room, and put it in her hand. She took it readily enough, and he reckoned she didn't want to be accepting favors because she was broke. It made him think of something he'd wondered many times. Why was it the man who was broke who had so much pride?

He lifted his glass and said, "Luck."

She made a half-hearted response to the toast before she put the glass to her lips. "Yeah, luck."

He smiled. "And all bad, huh?"

Her face went hard and she flicked a glance at him. She said, "I see my host, Mr. Higgins, has been telling you about the poor little whore who got pitched out by the other whores and ended up on his doorstep without the price of a penny candy."

He pursed his lips and said, lying, "Well, no, he didn't exactly say that. All he told me was you were a lady in some kind of distress—exactly what he didn't know. Said you seemed to have had some kind of argument or falling out with some other ladies you were traveling with."

She laughed. "Oh, bullshit. That old man didn't know what to think of the mess that landed in his lap. Me and that drunken bum that claimed to be a medical doctor." She laughed again and shook her head. "If it wasn't happening to me I'd think it was funny. I thought I'd come about as low as I could when I ended up stranded in Phoenix. But hell . . ." She looked around. "Right now Phoenix looks like paradise to me." She threw down the rest of her drink. "That is, if I ever get back there. I am busted. I don't have to price of a ticket."

Longarm cocked his head to one side and looked at her. "How come you were laying down? You sick or

33

something? Is that why the other working girls threw you out?''

"No." She shook her head. "They threw me out because I caused a ruckus when I found out how the split worked, what my end was going to be. Forty percent. Like hell." She shook her head again. "No, I didn't lay down because I'm sick. I haven't eaten in a couple of days and I was feeling weak. The old man's wife is a real nice lady." She suddenly looked up at Longarm. "But don't be telling them I'm hungry. I'm not taking any charity."

"You're going to accept a free ride back to Phoenix when the northbound stage gets here. What's that?"

She eyed him steadily for a moment. "I doubt you got the brains to follow this, but try," she said. "I had a ticket bought for me all the way to the south end of this line. I ain't come even halfway yet. I figure they still owe me about the same amount of miles it is back to Phoenix. Now, if you can get charity out of that, you're more than welcome."

He nodded his head slightly. "That's a nice bit of logic. Handy too. Especially when one has got more pride than sense."

She bristled. "What the hell are you talking about? Don't they owe me the miles or not?"

He smiled. "Yeah. But going south. If you want to be strict about it. You bought a southbound ticket. It entitles you to go south. Don't say nothing about north."

She gave him a level, fierce look. "Why don't you go to hell, fellow, whoever you are."

He said carelessly, "I'm the man who is going to give you a job to earn your way back to Phoenix. And maybe a few dollars more."

Her eyes narrowed. "What kind of job? On my back?"

He shook his head. "No, not quite. From time to time I'll need some things written down. That'll be your job. To write them down."

"Who in hell do you think you are kidding? You

34

know what I am. Don't talk to me about writing anything down. I know what you want down, and it's the underwear I got under this dress. Only you ain't going to get it.''

He nodded. "I don't want it. Under other circumstances and other conditions and maybe a different time, maybe yes. But not now and not under this set of circumstances. You savvy? So you can just get off acting like the hard-assed whore with me. You don't look like you ever put out for money in your life. I think this was your first try and you got scared and jumped ship.''

She was turning pink in the face. She said, "Say, just who in the hell are you? Did I ask you to tell my fortune? I've heard of a few folks got by just fine in life by minding their own business.''

"As to who I am, my name is Custis Long, if it makes any difference. And as to business, I'm offering you a job. Do you want it or not? It ain't got a damn thing to do with your clothes. In fact you will do all your business with me fully dressed. Understand that? Now, you want a job or not? I doubt there are many more around here. And this one pays cash.''

She narrowed her eyes. He noticed they were light blue. "You wouldn't be trying to offer me charity in a left-handed way, would you?''

He looked at her. She was trying to sit so proud and defiant, and not quite bringing it off. She was wearing a gray dress of some cheap gingham material, but she had a nice lace dicky around her collar. Or it would have been nice if it hadn't turned gray from the alkali dust. He said, "Listen, Rita, if that is your name, I wouldn't give you the sweat off a sow's snout without full return on my money. You'll welcome charity by the time I'm through with you.''

She didn't look quite so sure and some of the hardness had left her face. Relaxed, she was quite pretty. She had her hair pulled back in a bun, but he thought it would be about shoulder length and shining if she unpinned it and let it down. She said; "What-what would be my duties?"

He snapped it out. "Woman of all work. I say frog, you jump. Take down notes, fetch and carry, listen to my ideas and give me your opinion. Your duties are whatever I need at the time. Job is on the block. Going, going, go—"

"I'll take it!"

"Fine," he said. He reached into his pocket, pulled out his roll of bills, and peeled off a ten-dollar bill. He said, "Your first job is to go get me another drink." He handed her the bill. She took it hesitantly. "There's an advance on your salary. When you've brought me that drink you are to go look up Mrs. Higgins and buy you some lunch off her. And then—"

She jumped up. "So it was charity. By damn I—"

He reached out a hand and shoved her down. "Look, dammit, I can't have somebody working for me that is all weak in the knees from hunger. I don't want no more damn arguments from you. I'm a businessman. I own a large cattle company. I ain't used to my employees arguing with me. Now, do as you are told."

She got up slowly and took the glass out of his hand. She had a thoughtful look on her face. He watched as she walked over and went behind the plank bar. She hunted a moment, found the bottle of whiskey, and poured one of the glasses full. Then she looked across at him. "Am I supposed to have another one?"

"You're on my time now," he said, trying to sound severe. If the girl wanted convincing she had a job, he was going to be damn certain she got the message. He said, "You don't drink on my time. You work."

She nodded, and then brought the drink back across the room to him. As she handed it to him she held up the ten-dollar bill and said, "Am I supposed to pay Mrs. Higgins for the drinks when I buy myself some lunch?"

He shook his head. "I'm running an account with the old man. Besides, that is your money. That's an advance on your wages. I'm paying you five dollars a day until we get to Phoenix, and then we'll see what you're worth. Now go find Mrs. Higgins and see if she knows where that drunken doctor is. I want to get a look at him."

She gave him an amused look. "Going to give him a job too?"

He gave her a brief glance. "Ever notice how close those two words were? Hire and fire? Just one letter."

"I'm going," she said.

He watched with a faintly amused expression as she hurried from the room. But along with the amusement was an appreciation for the way her hips worked beneath the dowdy dress. He wondered if there were any clothes about that would fit her. He would like to see her better dressed. Also, he thought, he would like to see her completely undressed. He'd been out on the desert a long time, and it had been a spell since his last visit to his lady friend in Denver who was in the dressmaking business. He did not, however, think it would be a very good idea to take this Rita to his dress-shop lady and grandly ask her to fix the little gal up.

He remembered his boots, and walked over to where they were sitting by the door. He turned them upside down and a little water ran out. It was still too hot outside to put them in the sun, but he edged them out a little further where they might dry faster. He was getting tired of walking around in his stocking feet, and he figured it was just a matter of time before he picked up a splinter from the rough floor.

He took his drink to the table, and was just settling down to enjoy it and the stump of the cigar Higgins had given him when the door of the living quarters burst open and Higgins said excitedly, "It come. I got you a answer. All the way from Yuma."

Longarm waved his hand in a downward motion, and Higgins clamped his hand over his mouth. Longarm got up and walked across the room. Higgins said, "I'm right sorry. I jes' got so excited it burst right out."

"You got to watch that, Herman. Bursting out ain't no way to keep secrets."

37

"I got the message wrote down in here. I write a fair hand so you ought to be able to figure it out. Sounds mighty, mighty serious to me. This law work is deadly stuff, ain't it."

"Yes," Longarm said dryly. He followed Higgins into his front room and over to the desk. Higgins handed him a piece of paper with some words printed on it in pencil. The message said:

DEPUTY U.S. MARSHAL CUSTIS LONG

ALL ESCAPED PRISONERS ACCOUNTED FOR EXCEPT CARL LOWE. BELIEVE ONE OR TWO OF THOSE WHO AIDED ESCAPE MAY ALSO HAVE ELUDED ARREST. RANGERS CONTINUING SEARCH. BELIEVE LOWE MAY HAVE FLED TO THE SOUTH. ADVISE ANY DETAILS YOU MAY HAVE.

It was signed by the warden of the Yuma territorial prison. "Damn!" Longarm said. "Damn, damn, damn! I was afraid of that!" He wadded the piece of paper up and pitched it back on Higgins's little desk. "I told them he wouldn't head south! He's got no business in Mexico. That wasn't why they broke him out of prison!"

Higgins was standing by with his mouth open and his eyes wide. He said, "It's bad, is it, Marshal? Real bad?"

Longarm seemed to realize where he was. He looked at the little old man. He said, "Nothing for you to worry about, Herman. It's just law work. Law work gone wrong."

"Is they anything I can do?"

Longarm grimaced. "Not unless you can figure a way for me to get up in the Phoenix area. That's where I think I need to be."

"But didn't it say the chase was to the south?"

Longarm laughed. "Yeah. The chase. They're chasing their tails is the only chase they are involved with."

Higgins scratched his head. "I shore don't know no way for you to get north till the stage comes through."

Longarm shook his head. "You said something about grease, Herman. I need to try and get my boots back on."

Higgins frowned. "Might be yore feet need 'nother dose of lye water."

"Oh, I think I can do without that."

A little later he wandered outside to stand against the front wall of the stage station and stare out across the wasted prairie and think. His boots felt a little awkward and his feet were tender, but he felt nearly back to normal after his two-day trek across the barren plain. It was still hot enough to fry a bald man's brains, but the sun was heading down. In a couple of hours it would be twilight and cool.

Try as he would he could not think of any way to get hot on Carl Lowe's trail. The damn Arizona Rangers had insisted on hunting to the south. Otherwise, if they had taken Longarm's advice, Carl Lowe would be back in prison. But that was the damn Arizona Rangers for you. They figured every fugitive that was loose was going to break south for Mexico, especially in that part of the territory. Ordinarily that might be right, but Carl Lowe was no average outlaw. And the folks who had gone to some trouble to break him out of prison weren't going to take him to Mexico either. His skills would be wanted where there were some rich banks or railroad mail cars full of gold and cash. Longarm figured that had to be up north somewhere around Phoenix. That whoever had done it had broken Carl Lowe out for a purpose. Longarm had no doubt about that, and he had no doubt that the purpose involved a safe or a strongbox somewhere. And every hour Longarm sat out in the middle of the desert in a damned relay station was just that much more time he was getting behind.

He hunkered down, picked up a little stick, and began drawing a map in the sand showing where he was, where he had last seen Lowe, and the location of Phoenix and other places of opportunity. He was busy thinking of possibilities when Higgins came out. He looked ruffled and confused. Longarm asked him what was the matter.

He said, "My wife says that hoor is a-workin' fer you. I told her the sun had got to her. But I thought I'd come ask you."

Longarm laughed slightly. "It's a fact, Herman. Rita is my, uh—oh, I don't know—assistant I guess you'd call it."

Higgins looked slightly hurt. "I kind of thought me an' you was pretty much on top of thangs, Marshal Longarm. I didn't figure you to need other hired help."

Now Longarm did laugh. "You got it all wrong, Herman. She ain't working for me like you think."

But Higgins wasn't mollified. "I didn't see where we needed a hoor in the outfit. Was a woman needed, why, Sylvie would have fit right in."

Longarm frowned. He said, "You keep calling her a 'hoor,' Herman. You don't know that she is."

Higgins squatted in the sand across from Longarm. "Wa'l, she was in with a passel of hoors an' they run her off. What else I supposed to think?"

"You could have a horse in with a herd of cattle, but that wouldn't make a cow out of the horse, would it?"

Higgins reluctantly studied the question. Finally he took off his hat and scratched his head. "Wa'l, no, I reckon not."

Longarm said, "Look here, Herman, you got hold of the wrong end of the stick. The girl needed some help. She was weak because she hadn't eaten. I couldn't just walk up and hand her some money. She'd of thrown it back in my face. So I kind of made her up a job. She's my fetch-and-carry assistant." He put his hand on the old man's shoulder. "You're my thinking-and-action assistant. There's quite a bit of difference there."

Higgins's face brightened. "Aw, yeah. I see what you mean. Yeah, she is just yore fetch-and-carry girl. I get it now." He let out a high-pitched cackle. "Shore! Hell, you ain't a U.S. marshal fer nothin'." Then his face suddenly turned concerned. "Did you say that girl was weak on account of not eatin'?"

Longarm nodded. "Yeah. But I'd already figured that out."

Higgins protested. "But we offered her a meal. More than once. We shore did, Marshal. Whyn't she take it?"

Longarm shrugged. "Some people got more pride than they do sense. I could see it in her face minute I laid eyes on her."

Higgins looked pained. "That makes me feel right bad, knowin' they was a human being under my roof goin' hungry. Hell, I thought she was just stuck up and onery. She claimed we owed her a ride back to Phoenix 'cause she hadn't used the balance of her southbound ticket. I could see the logic in that, though it's agin company rules. But I was gonna bend them. I hate it she wouldn't take a meal with us, though. Hell, breakfast was just over when the coach come through and she got shoved off. My missus wouldn't thought nothin' of fixin' her a meal."

Longarm stood up. "Let's get out of this heat, Herman. What little fat I got is starting to sizzle."

"It is still a mite warm. I don't seem to notice it so much anymore."

Longarm touched Higgins's arm. He said, "Now, Rita doesn't know I'm a federal officer. You didn't let that out, did you?"

Higgins looked insulted. "Why, I reckon I didn't! What you take me for?"

"But you did tell your wife."

"Well, it so taken me by surprise 'bout you hirin' that girl that it jus' kind of come out natur—" He stopped and stared at Longarm, misery in his face. "Oh, I'm just a damned ol' fool. Thar I went and broke my word. Aw, hell!"

Longarm patted him on the back. "Doesn't matter. You'd of told her sooner or later. Wives just ain't happy until they know everything their husbands do."

Higgins said, "Ain't that a fact! You must be a married man yourself, Marshal."

Longarm said dryly, "Not very damn likely. But let's

just hold that information about me to you and your wife. Certainly we don't want Miss Rita to know.''

"You reckon her to be a good woman, Marshal?''

"I reckon her to be slightly confused right now. But then so am I.''

"How you gonna run down that outlaw you be after?''

Longarm shook his head. "I don't know, Herman. I just flat don't know. Or if I do, I don't know that I do.''

Chapter 3

Rita said, "What made you so sure I wasn't a prostitute? How did you know I hadn't been doing tricks on my back?"

Longarm laughed. "I've known a good many ladies in the trade, Rita, and they've all got certain charateristics. Mind you, I ain't running them down. I don't ordinarily have to pay for it, but I've given more than one respectable house a little of my patronage. And been well satisfied, I might add." He looked over at her with a small smile. "But you ain't nothing like them. I'm not saying you're better. Don't know you well enough to say that. All I'm saying is you don't play the part very well."

"How so?"

He laughed again. "Hell, Rita, it's—"

She broke in. "It's Rita Ann," she said. "I've always been called that. But the women I was in with thought it a good idea to drop the Ann. Said it made me sound kind of tame. But you ain't explained how you knew."

He shrugged. "Hell, it's obvious. Here you are in the middle of the desert, broke and hungry and not at all sure what you are going to do. Then I show up in your gunsights, the first real prospect you've seen. Higgins is out because his wife is right there. The doctor is drunk and probably broke. That leaves the two Mexicans, and you wouldn't have been ready for them. But here I was, and even if I wasn't dressed like a swell, I might have enough money in my pocket to get you out of your bind. A real whore would have been on me like a bad case of poison ivy. And as soon as you'd found out I had a few dollars to rub together, you'd have been rubbing yourself all over me and promising me the best time I'd ever had in my life. You'd have said your heart had just gone pitty-pat the second you laid eyes on me and you were still weak in the knees. But what did you do? Hell, you give me a look that would have burnt through saddle leather, and then turned your smart mouth on me when I offered you a drink and a little help. That ain't the way a whore acts, Rita.''

She gave a little laugh. "No, I guess not." She thought a moment. "But it's funny what you said about my heart doing a little flip-flop. When I saw you in the bedroom door that's kind of what happened to me. You were the best and the kindest-looking thing I'd seen in a long time. You looked like a gent."

"Must have been the hunger. You damn sure didn't act like it when you got up off that bed."

"It was because I had thought them things that I acted like that. Hell, I didn't know you. The last thing I needed was to get my fingers burned again."

"What do you mean by that?"

They were walking out in the early twilight, heading down toward the shack the Mexican mule handlers occupied. It was cool now that the sun was nearly down, and the sky had changed from a washed-out blue to an explosion of streaks of yellow and red and even deep purple. She said, tossing her head, "Oh, I don't know. It just seems like I never had no luck with men."

He stopped and looked at her. "Rita Ann, you ain't old enough to be making statements like that."

She sighed and heaved her shoulders. "Maybe it just

seems like it on account of this last little experience I had."

"Is that what put you in your present position, your last experience?"

She nodded. "Yeah, I suppose so." She looked up at him defensively. "But I'm not blaming anyone but myself, you understand. I'm twenty-two years old and old enough to account for my own mistakes."

"What kind of a mistake was it?"

She shrugged and looked away. "The stupid kind." She folded her arms under her breasts and hugged herself. "I was living in Saint Louis, living at home with my mother. My daddy had passed on. It wasn't a bad life. I had a good job waiting tables in the restaurant of one of the finest hotels in the city. And I had my share of beaus. They were kind of dull, but they were good young men. Then one day this man showed up at the hotel. All dashing and elegant and handsome as hell. He was a gambler. He'd just come off a riverboat on the Mississippi. Anyway, he took an interest in me, and after about two turns around the bed I was his toy. You couldn't have pried me loose from him with a crowbar. He said gambling on the river was finished, said the big money was out West and would I go. He said Phoenix or someplace like that. Said everybody out there had a pocketful of gold and no brains." She sighed. "So here we come. For a little while it was all right, but then he started losing. He never said nothing, but when he come in, late, he wasn't in no mood for anything except more booze. We kept changing hotels until we finally ended up in a boardinghouse. His temper got worse and worse, and then one day he was gone. Left me flat. Naturally I didn't have any money. Every nickel we had went for his stake, as he called it." She shrugged and dug at the sand with the toe of her slipper. "I felt like a damn fool. Woman in love. Hah! Damn. I had gone blind was what it was. All of a sudden those dull young men back in Saint Louis looked pretty damn good."

"So what did you do? Head for the nearest madam?"

45

She shook her head. "Not right away. I tried getting work waiting tables, but Phoenix is a rough town. Them hash houses in them places didn't want any little nice Rita Anns with nice manners. Slinging hash ain't just an expression, I found out. So I tried getting work cleaning houses. Whatever I could find. Nothing I could do paid anything. It was all I could do to earn enough to keep body and soul together, let alone earn enough for a train ride home."

"Couldn't you have wired your mother? Got her to send you some money?"

She gave him a look. "After the stunt I pulled? After walking out, running out, without so much as a good-bye? I don't know about your family, Mr. Long, but we got a little pride in mine. I done my mother wrong and I sure as hell wasn't going to turn to her for help after I'd made such a mess."

Longarm said, "I think I know how this story ends, but you might as well say the words."

She gave a laugh. "Yeah, I don't reckon it is so original. I finally decided I could starve to death sitting on it or I could sell it. So I went around to a local house and talked to the madam. She didn't have any cribs open, she said, but she knew about this crew of girls was going down south in Arizona near the border to relieve a crew that had been working down there for several months taking care of miners. I didn't even know where the damn place was. I don't know anything about this country except it could use a little water. Anyway, she sent me to this lady name of Rosy, and she put me in with five other girls was going down." She threw out her arms. "That's what I'm doing here."

"What caused them to throw you out of the stage?"

"*They* didn't throw me out. I *got* out. I got out when I found out all I was going to get was forty percent of the money I earned. If I charged ten dollars, I had to turn six into Rosy. That wasn't the way it was explained to me in Phoenix. So I said to hell with it. I'd been done

46

in by one bastard. I wasn't going to let some bitch do it to me also.''

"What made them think they could get away with it?''

She shrugged again. "Hell, they know you're broke. They knew I was green. Hell, they were going to have to teach me how to act. Seems that you don't make love when you're a whore the same way you do when you're just a woman. Said I was going to have to pay for the privilege. If they'd of told me that in Phoenix, I could have made my mind up and taken it or left it. But here they thought they had me over a barrel. Well, ain't nobody makes me do nothing I don't want to. I would have got out in the middle of the damn desert if it had come to it. I slugged Rosy a pretty good one. Split her lip for her.''

Longarm smothered a laugh. "But you are still here. Still a long way from Saint Louis.''

"You don't have to remind me.''

They had started walking again. They were walking by some corrals that were crowded with dun-colored Spanish mules. At the end of the corral was a rock shack. Smoke was curling out of the small chimney at one end of the cabin. Longarm said, "What about the doctor? How come he got pitched?''

She laughed dryly. "I don't know if he was drunk or out of his head or what. But a few hours before we got to here he announced that he was the doctor supposed to inspect all the girls to see if they had the clap or whatever. And then he commenced to give it a try right then and there on the stage. My word, you never saw such a ruckus. He was trying to get in under the skirt of this young girl—Wilda, I think her name was—and she was kicking and screaming and squirming around. Hell, you couldn't even see the doctor, if he is one, he had crawled so far up her skirt. Well, everybody piled in on him. Rosy has got a big old purse made out of cowhide, and she nearly beat him to death with it. The driver finally stopped and the guard came back and got matters straightened out. The doctor had lost his glasses and it took a time to find them. Rosy said that either the doctor got put off or they were getting off and just see how those miners at the other end of the line would like that. So the driver decided the doctor had to go. He tried to whine to me once we got here, but I didn't want no part of him.''

It had been Mrs. Higgins who had told Longarm where he might find the doctor. She'd said, ''Them Mexicans have got a big jug of either tequila or mescal, probably both. I reckon he's down there drinkin' with them. I don't think he's got much money. He inquired at the bar what whiskey cost, and when Herman told him four bits a shot, he kind of looked disappointed and wandered out the back. He's been down there around the Mexicans most of the day. Maybe he's swapping them some doctorin' for a little of that poison they drink.''

Now Longarm said to Rita Ann, ''You reckon he's a real doctor?''

She shrugged. ''I got no way of knowing. He's got a little black leather bag like doctors carry, but the only thing I seen him come out of that with was a bottle of whiskey. He never said much of anything until he went crazy and started that foolishness about examining the girls.'' She suddenly stopped. ''Say, what is your interest in the man? He's just a bum. What would a big cattleman care about him for?''

The question caught him off guard and for a moment he fumbled. ''Why, I don't know. Curious, I guess.''

''Curious about what? Some old drunk claims to be a doctor?''

He frowned. ''What the hell has got into you, Rita Ann? You seen me walking around in my stocking feet. You already know I nearly burned my boots off walking out of that desert. I kind of halfway hoped this man, if he is a doctor, might be able to do something about these blisters I still got. Might have some ointment of some kind.''

She put her hand to her mouth. She shook her head. "I don't know what gets into me sometimes. Here you been nothing but nice to me and I speak sharp to you. My mother always said this mouth of mine was going to get me in trouble."

He tried to put a light tone to it. "I reckon you forgot who was boss for a moment. Let's walk on. See if this man is still alive. If he's drinking mescal he might not be."

Ten yards further on they came to the little rock and adobe shack. The Mexicans were nowhere in sight, but a small man in a dirty black suit and a dusty white shirt and string tie was sitting on the ground by the front door. He looked up as they arrived. He was, Longarm noted, wearing wire-rimmed glasses that looked bent and barely held their perch on his nose. He put a finger to his glasses and pushed them up as he studied Longarm and Rita Ann from his sitting position. He had a quart bottle of what Longarm took to be mescal between his legs. It was not quite half full. The little man said, "Ah, visitors. Be welcome, be welcome. I am Doctor Amos Peabody, general surgeon and physician of Baltimore, Maryland."

Longarm looked down at him. "You're a long way from home, Doctor."

The little man nodded. "That I am, that I am." He made an effort to scramble to his feet, but only succeeded in reaching a kind of crouching position with his shoulder braced against the cabin wall. He peered at Rita Ann. "I do not believe I have had the pleasure of either the acquaintance of this young lady or yourself, sir."

Longarm noticed that he didn't slur his words, but he didn't seem to have a great deal of control over his body. He did, however, manage to keep one hand clamped around the neck of the mescal bottle. Longarm said, "No need to be formal, Doctor Peabody. I just had some sore feet and wondered if you might have any blister ointment, but I see you don't have your bag with you."

Doctor Peabody had gradually worked his way up to an erect position, though he was not deserting the support of the cabin wall. He said, "I have my bag, sir, certainly. No medical man would be without that necessary accessory. Unfortunately, I do not have the appropriate balm for your ailment. But I recommend goose grease, sir. Yessir, goose grease, finest remedy for irritated flesh."

Longarm laughed slightly. "They may have geese in Baltimore, Doctor, but ain't many in Arizona Territory."

"Of course not, of course not!" Doctor Peabody said. "What was I thinking? Then chicken fat. Yessir, chicken fat. And unless my ears have deceived me today, there are sounds of the very fowl somewhere about the place."

Longarm nodded at the bottle. "That mescal you're drinking, Doctor?"

Doctor Peabody held the bottle up and started as if surprised to find it in his hand. "By the heavens you are right, sir. Mescal it is. And home-brewed by the Mexicans who occupy this hutch. Fine stuff it is, sir. I'd offer you a drink, but I don't seem to have a clean glass. Or any glass for that matter." He looked vaguely around. Then he shoved the bottle toward Longarm. "Of course, if you don't mind a libation straight from the gourd, as the saying goes . . ."

Longarm shook his head and stepped back. "No, I reckon not, Doctor. That stuff is too strong for me." He stood a moment, studying the doctor's face. There was something wrong, but he couldn't put his finger on it. Certainly the doctor looked disreputable enough, with a several days' growth of whiskers on his face and his thinning hair awry and mussed. It was the eyes, Longarm thought. There was something not quite right about the man's eyes. But he couldn't see what it was. Maybe it was the way his glasses were teetering at such an odd angle. Maybe that was it. Rita Ann had said the doctor had lost his glasses in the scuffle. Maybe it was the bent frames. Longarm said, "Well, we'll let you get back to it, Doctor. Just wanted to see what you might have in the medicine line."

The doctor straightened himself a little more. "Be glad to have a look at your ailing members," he said. "Very nominal charge."

"No, I'm all right for now," Longarm said. He took Rita Ann by the arm and turned her away. "We'll be seeing you, Doctor."

But Peabody swayed away from the cabin wall and peered at Rita Ann over his crooked spectacles. He said, "This young lady, sir—I am being presumptuous, I know—but I have the most compelling feeling that I have had the pleasure of her company before."

Rita Ann said quickly, "Oh, I don't think so. I've never been to Baltimore."

The doctor scratched at his scraggly whiskers with his free hand and said, "My dear, the fair city of Baltimore hasn't been my abode in many a sorrowful year. No, I meant more recently." He swayed and caught himself against the wall.

Longarm said, "Reckon not, Doctor. You have yourself a real pleasant evening."

"And the best to you, sir, and your lady friend."

When they were far enough away Rita Ann said with a laugh, "The crazy old bastard doesn't remember that we were on the same coach for nearly a night and half a day."

"Maybe so," Longarm said thoughtfully. "Or he may well have known who you were. Something about the good doctor bothers me."

She laughed again. "Why should you give him a moment's notice? Heavens, that old drunk? Looks like he's been rolled in the dirt."

Longarm glanced at her gown. "Speaking of that. Ain't you got any other clothes? That gown makes you look like a widow. Ain't you got anything with a little color in it?"

She made a face. "My bag went with the coach. In the confusion and arguing I never did get it off. I guess it's nearly to Mexico now. I wore this dress on purpose. I didn't want to stir up any jealousy or hot blood from

51

anybody. I figured the less notice I called to myself the better off I'd be."

"How you going to get your bag back?"

"Mister Higgins was kind enough to wire down to the end of the line and ask them to send it back. I hope it arrives on that northbound stage day after tomorrow. If it doesn't . . ." She shrugged. "Every stitch I own is in there."

They had supper that night with Mr. and Mrs. Higgins in their quarters, eating at the little dining table in the outer room. Mrs. Higgins fixed chicken and dumplings, and topped it off with a peach cobbler she'd made out of canned peaches. Longarm pronounced it as maybe the finest meal he had ever had. And in a way it was, given the situation and the setting. Mrs. Higgins said, "Oh, how you do take on." But she pinked with pleasure and made sure his coffee cup stayed full.

Later he got her aside and talked about Rita Ann's plight. He said, "The poor girl is going around dressed like a street beggar or somebody about to go into a nunnery. That sure ain't calculated to lift her spirits. I know ya'll ain't of a size, but is they any chance you might have something she could cut down to fit her? I'd be more than glad to pay."

Mrs. Higgins said, "Let me think a minute." She wrinkled her brow for a time. Then she said, "You know, there was a Spanish woman through here a few years back. Spanish, not Mexican. She had to get off the coach on account of not feeling well. Had a world of luggage. If I remember right there was one case got left, and I think it had some gowns in it and maybe even some clean linen. We notified the company but they was never a word said or a claim put in. Now if I can just remember where I stored that valise."

While she was thinking, Longarm brought up the possibility of Rita Ann getting a bath. Mrs. Higgins just waved her hand. "Ain't nothin' to that. We got a cistern on top of the station here, and it feeds water down into

52

a little bathroom I got there at the back. Got a Sears and Roebuck galvanized tub. And the water won't need heatin'. Lord knows, it nearly gets up to boilin' during the day. Tell you what, you and the mister go out and have a drink. You send Rita Ann on back to me and we'll get something worked out.''

She stopped him as he was starting to turn away and said, with a twinkle in her eye, ''Gettin' sweet on the girl, are you?''

He gave her a wink. ''Sylvia, I been sweet on *all* the girls nearly all my life.''

''Well you send her on in here. We'll see what we can do.''

He and Higgins got themselves a drink at the bar, and then went and sat at the long table in the common room. Higgins, as if Longarm had led him to a great discovery, was drinking whiskey along with him. He said wonderingly, ''Why, I don't know whatever come over me to think that rum was so fine. Somebody must of sold me a bill of goods.'' He held up his glass of cheap whiskey. ''Now this is the real stuff, yessir, and I am much obliged for you straightening me out. Took a marshal of the federal government to do it, by golly, but it got done.''

Longarm had had an extremely difficult time getting Higgins to take twenty dollars in payment for his food and lodging. He'd finally fallen back on the lie that the government required him to pay for any services he received from civilians and that it was a breach of regulations if he didn't. Now he was faced with getting the stationkeeper to take another twenty for what Mrs. Higgins was doing for Rita Ann. His argument was that she had become his employee and as such, came under the regulations. After some argument Higgins finally accepted the additional money. Longarm said, ''Remember, Herman, I'll be riding free. The law allows me to do that. And you did send that telegram for me. It all works out pretty square all around.''

Higgins refilled their glasses and said, "You found that doctor, I take it?"

"Yeah. Name is Peabody."

"What'd you think?"

Longarm rubbed his jaw. "I ain't sure. He was slumped down on the ground and he looked kind of short and fat and mighty drunk. But then he stood up and he was bigger than I thought. Also, he don't talk so drunk. Course I have known hombres like that. Could drink whiskey until it was leaking out their ears and you'd never be able to tell it. But he kept looking younger the more I looked at him. I can't figure it." He suddenly laughed. "Told me to put goose grease on my feet."

Herman said, "Goose grease? Would chicken fat do as well?"

"He said that too, but my feet ain't feeling all that bad. I guess he's a doctor. He's mighty well spoken. Talks highfalutin as hell."

"I taken notice of that my own self. But I reckon he is going to have to sleep down there with them Mexicans. We ain't exactly set up for nightshirt company."

Longarm looked around. "I can sling my sleeping roll anywhere in here. If that is all right with you."

"That's mighty all right with me, Marshal. Onliest thang is I don't know where to put Miss Rita Ann."

Longarm said, "Well, I seen a divan in your front room. She ain't very big. Couldn't you give her a blanket and let her bed down on that?"

Higgins nodded. "Why, I don't see why not. 'Specially since she is connected to you."

"I'd be obliged."

Longarm calculated that they had been out in the common room drinking whiskey for about two hours when the door to the private quarters opened and Rita Ann came through followed by Mrs. Higgins. Longarm took a long look and said, "Well, now, that is more like it."

The dress Rita Ann was wearing was of definite Spanish origin, but it fit her like it had been made for her. It

54

was light blue and of some light, sleek material. It fit snugly around her waist and hips, and then flared out to a ruffled hem at the bottom. The bodice was a deep V cut, and the bosom of the dress was high, to lift Rita Ann's breasts so they looked bigger and more erect. Longarm stared at the V of white, very lightly tanned skin with just the hint of Rita Ann's breasts bulging into the opening. She had taken her hair down, and he saw it was a sleek, golden brown that caught the highlights from the kerosene lamps and threw them back.

Mrs. Higgins said, "Don't she look purty!"

Mr. Higgins said, "Why, I can't believe it's the same girl."

Rita Ann giggled. She said, "I'm just grateful to have a bath and be wearing clean underwear. Mrs. Higgins, I ain't ever going to be able to thank you."

Sylvia gave her a pat on the shoulder. "I never done nothin', Rita Ann. And them clothes have just been laying around here doing nobody no good." She said to Longarm, "There's another dress and a skirt and blouse. This was just the dressiest of the bunch, so we thought we'd give you boys a treat."

"It sure worked," Longarm said. To Rita Ann he said, "Sure makes a difference."

She walked over to him and whispered in his ear. "Yeah, but now I do feel like a hooker."

She was wearing just a hint of perfume. He said, "Well, you don't look like one. You look elegant. Mighty ladylike. And I'm glad to see you let your hair down."

She leaned against the far end of the plank bar. "I'm glad you approve. I always like to please the boss."

Higgins cleared his throat and got his big watch out of his vest pocket. He said, "Sylvie, do you know it is goin' on fer ten o'clock? It's a good ways past our bedtime. We can let Miss Rita Ann shake down on the divan, can't we?"

"Oh, my goodness, yes. I can fix that up real comfortable. I got a eiderdown quilt, dear, that is warmer than a good man on a cold night. But, Herman, if the—I mean, if *Mr.* Long is going to sleep out here, you better build him up a fire in the fireplace. This room gets mighty cold at night, Ma—" She had almost made the mistake twice and it flustered her. She said quickly, "I'll be goin' and gettin' your bedclothes, Rita Ann."

"I'll help."

Longarm helped Higgins put some big log chunks on the fireplace dogs and get it all lit. Higgins said, "They bring us the wood in from down south whenever anybody thinks 'bout it. Ain't much to be found hereabouts."

"I wouldn't reckon," Longarm said.

Higgins said, "I'm right sorry about the way my old woman nearly give the business away. I'll speak right sharp to her about that."

"No, don't. No harm done and she has been mighty nice. Besides, it may not matter about the girl knowing. I might tell her myself in a couple of days. Except then she won't take no more money from me."

"I'd better get to bed, Marshal. We rise right early here. But I reckon you do too."

Longarm walked back to the bar. "I'll be ready for the coffee before it stops brewing."

Higgins bade him good night, and then disappeared behind the door of his quarters. Longarm sat at the bar, nursing the last of a drink, wondering if Rita Ann would come out to bid him good night. Likely she wouldn't. She'd think that the Higginses would notice and might not approve.

He was surprised five minutes later to see the Higginses' door open and Rita Ann come through, closing it behind her. She came straight to him and leaned sideways against the bar, very near. He could smell that faint perfume she was wearing. She smiled. "Really like the dress?"

"I reckon," he said, his voice a little husky. He took a quick drink of whiskey, trying not to let his imagination get to work.

56

She said, "I'd like to thank you for what you've done for me."

He gave his head a quick shake, trying not to notice how the bosom of the dress cupped her breasts. He said, "No thanks needed. None wanted or expected."

"I still want to thank you." As she said it she leaned slightly closer.

He studied her for a second. "How, by punching my card?"

She frowned. "What?"

He shook his head quickly and poured some more whiskey in his glass. "Nothing. You want a drink?"

"No. I want to know what you meant."

In spite of her denial he pulled over a fresh glass and splashed a little whiskey in it for her, and then added some water out of a pitcher. He pushed it in front of her. He said, "It's nothing, just an old saying. Used to be a whorehouse down in Del Rio that would give cards out to their regular customers. Each card had ten little boxes on it, and every time a customer would come in the lady he was with would punch out one of the boxes, punch his card. When he had ten boxes punched the next time was free." He shrugged. "I shouldn't have said it."

She was still frowning. "You damn sure shouldn't have."

He gave her a look. "You come out a while ago and said you felt like a hooker. I didn't know it was such a touchy subject."

"I was trying to tell you I wanted to thank you."

"Well, how the hell else was I supposed to figure you meant it? What was you going to do, come over and offer to oil my saddle?"

"For all you know, I was going to offer to wash your shirts."

"Mrs. Higgins already done that."

"Oh? And what did you do for Mrs. Higgins?"

He looked around quickly. She had a small smile on her face. It made her look younger than she was. He

57

said, "You over your little pout?"

She moved close enough that she could put her arms around his shoulders and cup her hands behind his neck. But she made no move to bring her face closer to his. She said, "I can't figure out who the hell you are."

He looked away. "I told you. I'm a businessman in the cattle trade."

"No, you're not. I've known businessmen and you're not a thing like them. You've got too much of an air of, of authority about you. Even I can feel it, and Mr. and Mrs. Higgins act like you hung the moon. You act like a man used to giving orders and having them obeyed. Are you some kind of boss of this stage line?"

He shook his head. "No. I'm sure not. I'm no more to this stage line than you are."

"Then how come Mr. Higgins uses the telegraph for you?"

"He used it for you, didn't he? Wired about your bag."

"Yeah, but I didn't tell him what to say and he didn't come running when he got an answer." She wrinkled her brow. "You're somebody. I just don't know who. I could tell that even Peabody felt it, the way he got to his feet."

"That was for you. Standing for a lady."

"No. He didn't get up until you started talking."

He sighed. "Lady, you got you some kind of a big imagination."

"Maybe," she said. "And maybe not. I may not be the smartest thing on two feet, but I ain't just come to town for the county fair either."

"Drink your drink."

"Are you going to let me thank you?"

He turned and looked into her eyes. They were light gray, hard to see clearly in the lamplight. It made him think of Doctor Peabody's eyes. He still hadn't figured out what was wrong with them. But he put Peabody out of his mind. This girl was here and very close. He could smell and feel the femaleness of her. He said, "Take a

58

look around. You see any place private? And so far as outside, I don't know about you but I ain't going to take my clothes off out there. It's cold as a well-digger's ass. Besides, I've told you you don't owe me anything.''

She leaned her head closer, bringing her face only a few inches from his. ''What if I was to tell you that it ain't got nothing to do with thanks. What if I was to tell you it was me. I told you I got that feeling the first time I saw you.''

He jerked his head away. ''I appreciate the thought, but I invite you to look around again. Ain't much privacy here.''

She smiled. ''Oh, I reckon something can be worked out. Where you going to spread your bedroll?''

He nodded toward the far back corner where the fireplace was. There was about a six-foot space between the end of the big table and the roaring fire. He said, ''Why, over there. Why?''

''You want me to help you spread your roll?''

He shook his head. ''I been able to do that for myself for quite a long time. Never needed no help before.''

''I think you need help. And I'm the girl can give it.'' She brought her lips to his. Gently her tongue forced its way into his mouth, and her arms tightened around his neck. For a long moment they kissed. He could feel a pounding in his temple and feel desire rising through his body. When she pulled back he was panting slightly. He said, ''What in hell did you do that for? Get me all aroused and then nothing can be done. Hell!''

''We'll see,'' she said. She leaned down and kissed him again, a brief but passionate kiss that brought his arousal up another notch. Then she stepped back. ''Put your bedroll down. Sleep tight.''

He felt the light touch of her hands on the back of his neck disappear, and then, before he could reach out for her, she had turned and was gone. In a few steps she reached the door to the Higginses' living quarters, opened the door, and slipped inside. He saw the door firmly close behind her. ''Son of a bitch!'' he said in a

59

half whisper. She had left him feeling like an unexploded firecracker. Taken all in all, he'd just as soon she'd kept her match to herself and not lit his fuse if she wasn't going to take it all the way. But then, he thought, maybe she intended that the kiss be her thanks. If that was the case, she set a mighty high store by her kisses.

He said "Hell!" out loud, and then turned his glass up and finished his drink. Hers sat untouched. It was watered, but he didn't care. He took it down in two gulps, and then got off the high stool he'd been sitting on. It was late. And getting later. The best thing he could do was spread his bedroll and get what sleep he could. He crossed to his saddle, untied his rolled blankets, and took them and his saddle over in front of the fire. The stones of the fireplace were just starting to heat up and spread warmth. It felt good. The inside of the station had grown cold as the night had worn on.

He got his blankets arranged to where he was in the shadow of the end of the table and a couple of yards from the fire. He didn't want to get too warm at first and then freeze when the fire burned down. He set his saddle at the end of his bedroll for a pillow. After that he looked around. There were still two lanterns burning, and he went to each and turned down the wick until they went out. Then, by the light of the fireplace, he went back to his bed, sat down on the hard floor, and took his boots off. He was pleased that his feet were not as tender as he had expected. He thought, however, that he would leave his socks on for extra protection.

He took off his gunbelt and laid it carefully beside his saddle. His gunbelt featured a big silver concave belt buckle. It was big and it was concave for a reason. Inside the buckle, held by a steel clip, was a two-shot .38-caliber derringer. He made sure the little gun was still secured safely before he tucked the gunbelt half under his saddle with the big Colt .44-caliber revolver with the six-inch barrel sticking out where it was quick to hand. After that he took off his hat and his shirt and laid them ready to hand. He unbuckled the belt that held up his jeans and unbuttoned the first few buttons, but he didn't take them off. Normally he would have slept naked, but he might not be up and dressed before the Higginses came out. Even though he wouldn't be as comfortable, he figured it was better to at least keep his pants on. He got under two blankets with just one and his slicker between the hard, wooden floor. It didn't much matter to him. He could sleep on the top of a flagpole if he was tired enough, and he was plenty tired after his trip across the desert.

He got himself settled, lying on his side, facing the fire. Normally he went right off to sleep, but the girl was bothering him. She could have gone a month or more without getting him as fired up as she had. Well, he thought, maybe she didn't know any better and was just trying to be nice. And then there was always Phoenix. They would both be heading in that direction, and a good opportunity might present itself to take the situation beyond a kiss that had been like liquid fire.

He squirmed around and tried to turn his mind in a different direction. He thought of Carl Lowe, wondering where he was and just what job he had been broken out of prison to perform. Maybe he hadn't been assisted in the break, and even if he had, maybe it hadn't been for a purpose. But Longarm was damn hard pressed to believe anything to the contrary. Somewhere, someplace up the road was a safe or a strongbox just waiting for Carl Lowe's touch. Longarm felt extremely frustrated that all he could do was lie on the floor in a relay station and wait.

And then there was Doctor Peabody. Longarm could not imagine anyone, even a doctor from Baltimore, Maryland, trying to perform an examination on a passel of whores in a moving stage in the middle of the Arizona badlands. And doing it just before they were to get to a relay station where he could be conveniently put off the stage. He was supposed to have been drunk, but Longarm didn't believe that anyone ever got that drunk.

He lifted his head off his saddle and shook it. Hell,

either he'd had too much of Higgins's bad whiskey, or he was getting an imagination like a five-year-old kid. He was jumpy, sure enough, and Miss Rita Ann hadn't helped matters in the slightest with her kiss and her promise. Hell!

Just then a movement caught his eye in the dark. He raised his head again, peering through the dim light. He thought he'd seen the door to the Higginses' quarters open, but his angle of view was bad.

Then something loomed into his vision. For a second he thought it was Mrs. Higgins. Then she spoke softly, and he realized it was Rita Ann, obviously wearing one of Mrs. Higgins's sleeping gowns.

She came to the edge of his bedroll and looked down at him. "I couldn't sleep."

Then, as he stared mesmerized, she slowly pulled the flannel nightgown over her head and stood there before him, naked in the flickering firelight.

Chapter 4

In the glow of the flickering fire he could see her white skin as it was touched here and there by light and shadow. She started to kneel down beside him, but he said, "No, don't. Stay like that for a moment. I want to look at you."

He sat up, the blankets falling down to his waist, and his eyes focused on her. He let his eyes travel up and down her, savoring her erect breasts that were about the size of small grapefruits. But they came quickly to a shapely point, ending in small, dark nipples set in big, round rosettes. When the fire blazed up, he could see that they were crinkling and puckering, either with the chill of the air or with her excitement.

Her legs were long and straight. She was standing with them apart so that the place where they met ended in a little inverted U rather than a V. The V was her auburn-colored bush that ran at least three or four inches up her belly.

She said, "I'm cold."

He threw the covers back.

She said, pointing, "You've got your jeans on. I thought you'd be ready."

As fast as he could he unbuttoned the last of the but-

63

tons, and then began shucking his pants. She said, "What about your underwear?"

"Don't wear any."

"That's good." She knelt down beside him, took the end of the legs of his jeans, and jerked them off. Then carefully, she put her hand on his chest and pushed him back. She said, "You just lay there. I want to do this the way I like."

They were both whispering. He said, "What about the Higginses?"

"They're snoring. You just lay there and let me do it. You don't yell, do you?"

He was starting to have to grit his teeth, the desire was rising so strong in him. He could smell the musk of her even though she was three feet from his nose. He lay back with his head on the seat of his saddle. By looking over his cheekbones he could just see what she was doing. She had straddled his legs, down just above his ankles. He saw her bend over, and then a delicious thrill ran all through him, making him shudder, as she took him in her mouth. He let out a long, low "Aaaaaaaah."

She lifted her head. "You like that?"

"Oh, yes," he said in a hoarse whisper. "Oh, yes, oh, yes."

She whispered, "You'll like this too."

He felt his testicles suddenly go warm, and then felt sensations shooting through them, each in turn, as she took them in her mouth and bathed them with her tongue. He let out another sigh, straining to keep it as quiet as he could. He said, whispering, "You better not do too much of that."

And then she was taking his member in her mouth again and slowly rotating her lips up and down it, and then half around and then back half around. He could feel himself swelling toward a climax. With an effort he fought down the feeling. "Oh," he said, to warn her. "Oh, oh, oh."

Silently she went to all fours and crept up his body.

She came up to his face and lowered her lips to his, and for a moment locked him with her mouth and her tongue. He tried to put his arms around her, but she pushed them down. It was clear she wanted to do it exactly as she wished. He lay there, his arms at his side, the ache in his groin growing, the pounding in his temple increasing, the desire inside him about to burst out.

Then she slowly started back down him, kissing his chest and then his stomach as she moved. Finally she stopped and raised up. He could clearly see the curly thatch that protected the pink insides of her vagina right over his member. Then, with a quick movement of her hand, she guided him inside her and settled down on him, taking all of him, taking him into her wetness and warmth. He let out a gasp and clenched his fists. Then, supported on her knees, she began to grind up and down and around, sometimes going slow and then suddenly making little short quick bursts up and down. All the time she held his eyes with hers, a slight smile playing on her lips.

It was as if she could feel when he was just about to explode. Just as he'd reach the top, feeling there was no stopping, she'd suddenly cease her motion and hold very still, watching him. When it seemed he had subsided, she would start bringing him back up again. The fire was warm, but it was not the heat from the fire that was putting sweat on his face. He had never felt such delicious, painful ecstasy in all his life. The woman was playing him like a cat would a mouse.

She suddenly went through a quick series of grinds and then a burst of thrusts. He opened his mouth, about to make a soundless scream, when she abruptly stopped. He thought that now he would really scream, with anguish. He couldn't take it any longer. And then she smiled. She said, "Now!"

But she didn't move her hips. Instead, she somehow began milking him with the muscles she had inside her vagina, pulling him up and pushing him down. Squeezing him and releasing him. He was so sensitized that it took no more than a half a minute of the massaging before the world suddenly went black and then exploded in a torrent of flashes of yellow and red and orange. He could feel himself tumbling, quivering, shaking, rolling over and over and over. He could feel himself thrusting his middle toward the sky, trying to reach some unattainable target in the heavens. He strained and he strained and he strained.

Then, spent, he suddenly slumped back. For a second his head whirled, so that he didn't know up from down or front from back. But a few seconds later he opened his eyes. He was panting hard, but other than that, seemed unhurt. She was smiling down at him. "Did that feel good?"

He was too short of breath to speak. All he could do was croak, "Goodness! My goodness."

She leaned forward and kissed him softly on the lips. "Good night."

Before he could say a word she was suddenly gone. He turned his head just in time to catch the motion of the Higginses' door opening and closing. She was gone. Only the scent of her musk lingered to prove that she had been there.

He lay still for a few moments, slowly coming back to himself. He finally realized he was freezing to death with the blankets thrown back and his bare skin exposed to the chilly air. He jumped up, took two small logs off the wood stack, and threw them on the fire, jumping out of the way of the shower of sparks. Then, as quickly as he could, he pulled his jeans on, not bothering to button them back up. Finally he lay down and got under his two blankets. He laid his head back on the seat of his saddle and stared up at the ceiling, now visible by the glow from the replenished fire. Hell, he thought, did I dream that? Was she really out here? Did she just milk me and milk me dry? Did I ever even touch her? His hands ached for the feel of her breasts, her belly, her thatch, the warmth and caress of her vagina. But they were empty. He had touched her with his eyes and his

66

imagination, but nothing else. She had been the ring-master. All he'd done was lay back and be astonished.

He shook his head. The girl was no hooker, but if she wanted to be she could make a fortune. He'd never known a woman who could do what Rita Ann could. She could tease you and tempt you and hold your hand just away from the cookie plate, and then, all of a sudden, gorge you until you didn't think anymore. She was truly something. He remembered her in the gray gown, remembered thinking how unremarkable and almost dowdy she'd seemed, about as exciting as an old-maid schoolteacher. Well, he wasn't going to think that anymore.

With an effort he took his mind off her and turned on his side and forced his mind to go blank. As it was he was dead for sleep and, even if he hurried, he was probably going to get no more than five hours' worth.

He awoke to the sound of someone moving around on the floor near his bed. He opened his eyes carefully, not sure for a second where he was or what time it was. He saw a pair of boots and then some old khaki pants, and looked up. It was Higgins putting more logs on the fire. He could see that it was still dark out, but the old man appeared to be up for the morning. Longarm sat up, rubbing at his eyes.

Higgins said, "Marshal, you awake? Hope I didn't wake you up slinging these blamed logs around, but the old woman wanted this part of the place warmed up before her and the girl come out. She thought we'd all eat breakfast out here."

"What time is it?" Longarm's mouth felt like glue. "Hell, I was sleeping hard."

" 'Bout half past five. But you can nod on off again if you be a mind. It'll be a good half a hour 'fore Sylvie can get breakfast fixed. Though she's got Rita Ann a-he'pin' her. That's a right pert girl, you know that?"

"Yeah," Longarm said. He yawned. Higgins was dressed in the tops of his long underwear with just his

67

suspenders to hold up the old pair of pants he was wearing. The fire was heating up, and Longarm threw back the covers and went to hunting for his socks. When he'd found them, he pulled one on each foot and then put on his boots. He picked up his shirt and stood up. "I better move my bedroll before you set it on fire."

Higgins looked around quickly. "I gettin' fahr on you?"

"Naw. I just said it for a good excuse to get my old bones moving." He began rolling up his blankets and slicker. He said, "Wonder about the doctor."

"What about the doctor?"

"Wonder where he slept."

Higgins turned around. "With the Mexicans, I'd reckon. I made it plain as paint to him that we wasn't no hotel an' didn't have no room fer overnight guests. Said he was welcome to as much of the prairie as he could occupy."

"Wonder what he thought about me and Rita Ann."

Higgins turned away, dusting his hands. "Wa'l, that wouldn't be any of his business. He come in here like a fine gentleman like yoreself an' matters might of been different. But he staggers round here tryin' to get free whiskey, he can go to blazes for all I care. I reckon we'll eat on this end of the table, close to the fire. It won't be quite sunup by the time Sylvie gets it on the table. And shore as hell won't have warmed up none."

"Wonder how the doctor made out last night. It was some cold, I would reckon."

"Pshaw!" Higgins said. "Tanked up as he was, he'd of melted a heavy snowfall. Nosir, that man couldn't have frozen in a snowbank. I wouldn't go to lightin' no matches around him. Nosiree, Bob. An' if he was in here I'd make damn sure he never got close to the fahr."

Longarm walked over close to the bar to get away from the now-roaring fire. He expected that Higgins had either gotten caught up in his own words and forgotten what he was doing, or was planning on heating the outside as well. The bottle of whiskey was sitting where he'd left it the night before, and even though it wasn't daylight yet, he poured a little in a glass, added some water, and then took a mouthful and swished it around to clean his mouth up a little. He'd have liked to wash his face and the back of his neck, but the only water was at the back of the Higginses' bedroom, and that was blocked off by whatever the ladies were doing.

He said to Higgins, "Don't you reckon you ought to open the front door?"

The old man came over, sweating lightly. "What would I want to do that for?"

"Might be a rattlesnake out there is about froze. Might save his life."

Higgins wheeled around and looked at the fire. "You know, I might have got that blaze built up a little. By golly, you are right. Gonna be too hot to eat at that end of the table. I reckon I had better open the front door. Let some air in here to mix around."

He had barely gotten it open when Sylvia and Rita Ann came out of the household quarters, each of them carrying a platter. Higgins had lit several lamps, and Longarm got a good look at Rita Ann. She was wearing a flowered skirt and a plain white short-sleeved blouse. The skirt was short, coming just above her knees, and the blouse was of a thin material and tight, accentuating the shape and erectness of her breasts. She gave Longarm a sly smile and said, "Good morning, Mr. Long."

"Good morning," he said. He stared at her, thinking of how she'd looked in the gray dress the day before and then how she'd been that night. She was like a stick of dynamite, just lying there in a brown paper wrapper until you set it off. And then you got the surprise. And the explosion. And the fireworks. He kept staring at her, hoping she'd make some kind of sign so he'd be certain he hadn't dreamed the night before, but she went serenely on with helping Mrs. Higgins lay breakfast.

Mrs Higgins said, "Herman, whatever has possessed you?" She was fanning herself with an empty plate. "I thought it was hot in that kitchen but, laws, you have

69

set the very fires of Hell loose in this place!''

Higgins looked guilty. "I got the front door open. She'll cool off right quick."

"Well, we can't eat till it does. Laws, a person couldn't put a bite of food in their mouth in such heat. Wouldn't be healthy.''

Longarm went over to his saddlebags and got out his toothbrush and a bar of soap. He asked Mrs. Higgins if he might go in the bathroom and clean up a little.

She said, "Why, bless you, yes. Rita Ann will show you where they's some bakin' soda and salt for your teeth, won't you, dear?''

Rita Ann looked over at Longarm. "I'd be right happy to," she said.

He followed her through the door and into the Higginses' quarters, and then through the second door and the bedroom. There was a small door off to the right that he had never noticed before. She led him into a little shack that he guessed had been added on to the main building. It was half bathroom and half kitchen, separated by a blanket curtain. The kitchen had a big cast-iron range and a sink set in the middle of drainboards and sideboards that ran the length of the little room. She led him over to the sink, which was armed with a water pump. With a lithe motion she reached up in a cupboard and came down with a box of salt and another of baking soda. To that she added a glass. While she pumped the glass full she turned to him with a smile and said, "How did you sleep last night, Mister Long?''

He said dryly, "I had the feeling something rousted me out around midnight. I can't be sure because it came and went so fast.''

She handed him the glass. "I didn't think it came so fast. Maybe left quick.''

He gave her a look, and dipped his toothbrush in the water and then in the soda and the salt. She was standing very near him, with the both of them facing each other while turned sideways to the sink. Without looking, she reached down and unbuttoned the middle buttons of his

70

jeans and thrust her hand in. He had the toothbrush in his mouth, and could only jerk and make a muffled sound in surprise. Still looking him straight in the face, she began to fondle him. He could feel himself becoming aroused, feel the swelling starting like a rutting bull. He took the brush out of his mouth and said, "Rita Ann, are you crazy? Mrs. Higgins could come in at any second."

But she paid him no heed. All of a sudden she dropped to her knees and took him in her mouth. He gasped and almost bit the end off his toothbrush. His mouth was full of soda and salt and he was suddenly gasping for breath.

Holding him firmly by the backs of his thighs, she began to piston her head back and forth, taking his whole member inside her mouth with each stroke. He gasped and flung his toothbrush on the counter and looked down. Her blouse had gaped open, and he could see her firm breasts tipped with the small nipples like raspberries. He put his hands on her head, making a halfhearted attempt to stop her, but it was too late. He could feel the crescendo of passion rising and rising in him until there was no way to stop it. He was gasping for air, clutching at her fine, silken hair. He said, "Rita Ann—you've got to—" He never finished. The fire she had set blew out of control and the whole mountain went up, erupting as the streaks of red and yellow and orange flames flashed in front of his eyes. He sagged sideways, clutching at the counter for support, too weak to stand on his feet.

A time passed. It could have been a moment, it could have been ten minutes. He didn't know. The next thing he knew she was standing up, putting him back in his jeans, and buttoning him up. She said, as he gasped and hung on to the counter, "You better hurry up and wash up or you'll be late for breakfast. I've got to get these biscuits out of the oven and out to the table." Then she gave him a quick kiss on the cheek. While he hung on, his breathing gradually returning to normal, he heard the

71

oven door clang and then she was calling out as she left, "Hurry up now, Mr. Long. They got honey to go with the biscuits. I sure hope it has cooled off in there."

When he could, he straightened up and looked toward the door through which she had disappeared. She was, he thought, the damnedest woman he'd ever run into. She left him completely flummoxed. What she'd done to him had been done before, but never in the kitchen, and never when he was trying to brush his teeth, and never with two other people waiting breakfast. "Son of a bitch!" he said out loud. "Between carrying in the bacon and the biscuits."

It was still too hot, and they had to eat at the far end of the table down near the door. It was just coming daylight as they sat down to the meal. They had something Mrs. Higgins called "egg loaf." It was a lot of eggs mixed with some flour and baking powder and a little milk and then baked. It was served by the big spoonful. Longarm thought it was good, though he could have done just as well with plain fried eggs. But Higgins raved about it, so Longarm figured that was why it was on the menu. They had thick slices of bacon and biscuits with honey. There was also cream for their coffee. Mrs. Higgins said, "We keep three milk cows, but it's so hard gettin' the company to send down enough of the right kind of feed and hay that one or the other of 'em is always going dry."

Longarm ate, but he also spent a good deal of time staring at Rita Ann. Mrs. Higgins said, "I tell you, this girl is just a joy. Help around the kitchen? My goodness, you have no idea how good she is in that kitchen."

Oh, yes I do, Longarm thought silently. But he said, staring at Rita Ann, "Is that right?"

"Just like the daughter I never had."

"Daughters can be just full of surprises," Longarm said, still looking at Rita Ann. She smiled back at him, and then reached over and poured his coffee cup full.

When the meal was over, Longarm took his coffee

and went over to the bar and drank off enough to where he could put a fair amount of whiskey in it. Then he returned to the table. The women were up and clearing away. Higgins was relaxing with his own cup, sweetened with honey. He said, nodding toward Longarm's coffee, "I can't take the whiskey right off. It goes agin my stomach."

Longarm took a sip. It had become clear daylight outside and the sun was already making its presence felt. If Higgins's fire didn't die down soon, the combination of the two would make it mighty warm in the room. Longarm said, "It's a bad habit. But I've got myself so stove up over the years, takes a little doing to get my old bones to moving. I guess I use the whiskey about like you'd use liniment. Or a switch to a mule."

Higgins looked toward the door. "Going to be a hot one."

"Now when exactly is that northbound stage due?"

"Supposed to get in here tomorrow at three in the afternoon. Course they never do. But they generally run pretty close, half an hour, give or take."

Longarm studied his coffee cup. "Mr. Higgins, I want to ask you a question I know you are not supposed to answer, but I got to ask it and you got to answer because it is government business. Does your stage line carry gold bullion?"

Higgins laughed. "I can answer that easy enough. Lord, yes. Don't you see, that was the whole purpose why the line was set up. Passengers is just a kind of extra freight. Not that we don't carry considerable freight. We do. Sometimes they'll hook up two stages in tandem and put maybe twenty mules on and carry a passel of freight."

"So they ship bullion? Pure bullion?"

"Yessir. Smelted down right there at the mine so's to make it as small a load as possible. They tell me they even get the silver outten it so's it be pure gold."

"How long has this been going on?"

Higgins shook his head. "Wa'l I can't say prezactly,

73

but a good little while. Three, four years. Soon as them mines down there in them mountains close to the border commenced paying off, why, the company went to thrashing around to find a way to get the gold north to the mint to sell it to the government. I believe they first off tried sending it in armed caravans, but that never worked. Might as well have held up a sign tellin' the world they was transporting gold. Mexican bandits liked to have got fat off such stunts. Lot of men got killed. Finally the company set up this stage line. Course they'd of much rather had a railroad, but ain't nobody got the money to lay track across some of that country. So they started in the stage business.''

Longarm said, ''And the idea is that nobody knows which run is carrying the gold, is that about right?''

The old man nodded. ''Ain't no flies on you, Marshal. But that ain't the biggest trick. The strongbox they send it in is what is the tough nut to crack. Why, they ain't a chisel made can get through that hardened steel. Hell, the safe itself weighs near five hundred pounds, and you add a half million dollars worth of gold to that and you got yourself a load. Ain't ten men, if everyone of 'em could get a holt, could lift it. And ain't no way to get past the lock. Nosir. They got a key down yonder they lock it with and one up yonder in Buckeye they unlock it with. In between times she stays shut tighter'n an old maid's cookie jar.''

Longarm thought, unless you have a Mr. Carl Lowe handy. But he said, ''How can the stage handle that kind of weight?''

''They built for it. Extra stout with extra wide-rimmed wheels.''

''Don't the ones bearing the gold cut a deeper track?''

Higgins laughed. ''Ever' one of them stages is carrying a safe. And ever' safe has got something in it. Some of 'em got gold inside and some of 'em got a load of lead.'' He gave Longarm a wink. ''Ain't no flies on them folks pays me a salary. That's why we use such big teams and have the relay stations so close together.

74

Regular stage might use just four mules, maybe six, and put the stations forty miles apart before they changed teams. Nosir, this here is a first-class outfit.''

"You ever been held up?''

Higgins said, "Well, I can't speak about that, Marshal, because I don't know. But I do know that the company let it be advertised far and wide what kind of safes they were using and just what a tough nut they were. Newspapers carried articles about how the safes had to be loaded and unloaded with a block and tackle. What's the good of holding up one of our stages if you can't make off with the goods?''

Not, Longarm thought to himself, unless you've got a man who can open the safe on the spot and then all you got to transport is the gold. It made sense to him. The only problem was that he didn't have the slightest idea where Carl Lowe was or when he and his gang, and Longarm had no doubt a gang of some kind had been formed, intended to strike.

"Who knows there is gold being loaded down at the south end?''

"Well, I don't exactly know the who.''

"Do you know when a shipment is coming through? I'm just asking.''

"Good heavens, no! My stars and garters. Ain't but damn few knows that. None of the drivers or guards knows. I guess the men who load it up know, but they don't know till the last minute, and I've heard they get locked up for the next twenty-four hours after they've built a load. Course that may just be talk.''

"Then who does know?''

"Well, I reckon they is two or three fellers down in the south knows. And then they is a couple up in Buckeye on the lookout fer it. Least that is what I heered.''

"How do they know?''

Higgins sipped at his coffee and picked at bread and biscuit crumbs on the table. "They say they wire up from the south to the folks in Buckeye. But that's just talk.''

"But wouldn't that put the word out? Telegraphing like that? Everybody on the line would know."

"Aw, they supposed to use some kind of code. They is messages goin' back and forth all the time so you never know which one is about the gold. They might wire up to Buckeye and say they is runnin' short on pickaxes and that might be the signal the gold is going the next run."

Longarm drained his cup and stood up. He said, "Herman, I got a bad feeling that the stage coming in tomorrow is not carrying lead bars."

Higgins looked instantly distressed. "Aw, no. I shore hope it is. Seein' as you and Miss Rita Ann gonna be on that stage. You shore?"

Longarm shook his head. "A hunch. Just a hunch. But it is a strong one."

"What had we better get to doing?"

Longarm smiled. "Nothing I know of, Herman. It's just a hunch. I'm not recommending you wire down to the border and tell them to hold off. Frankly, it's mainly about that fellow I had you telegraph about. The one broke out of prison. He's got me jumpy. Likely I am fighting my head. I wouldn't worry about it."

Higgins stared at him for a second. "Man says they is a rattlesnake likely loose in the house, an' then says not to worry. My stars and garters, Marshal, robbin' means guns and guns means killin'. I got my old woman to worry about."

Longarm shook his head. "If there is any robbery planned, it won't be done at a relay station. It'll take place out yonder, out in the big middle of nowhere, so there aren't any witnesses. But get it out of your mind, Herman. Besides, I'm here."

Herman nodded his head slowly. "Yep. That you are, Marshal. For which I thank my lucky stars."

The morning passed slowly. Longarm saw very little of Rita Ann. She seemed occupied in the back with Mrs. Higgins, sewing or something. Higgins said they were working on the clothes the Spanish lady had left to make them a better fit. "You know them women. Get a needle in their hand and a piece of cloth and nothin' won't do till they've changed it all about."

Mid-morning Longarm walked outside for a look around. He walked to the back and saw the two Mexicans working with the mules, sorting them out. He figured it was a considerable job adjusting harness for that many mules. Not that they were of a much different size. As a bunch they were pretty uniform, but there was no harness made that would fit all the mules in a team. Longarm figured the Mexicans tried to keep them bunched as to size, but that also was not such an easy task because he knew that a team, even horses, had to be temperamentally suited, and if they weren't, they would never pull together.

He walked over to the corral fence and watched the Mexicans working. It was clear they knew exactly what they were doing, and they did it with an economy of motion and as little excitement to the animals as possible. Up close the mules looked bigger. Longarm knew that most people thought of Spanish mules as small up against, say, a saddle horse. But they weren't that much smaller. A big horse might weigh eleven or twelve hundred pounds, with the majority being closer to a thousand. But he calculated that the mules, the majority of them, were not much more than a hundred pounds less than that. And mules, for some reason, were stronger than horses. They weren't as fast, but they could outlast and outwork nearly any horse you put one up against.

Longarm looked down the fence line to the shack. He didn't see Doctor Peabody. Likely he was inside either nursing a hangover or nursing the bottle of mescal. Maybe both. He wondered what kind of arrangements the little man had made with the Mexicans to take him in. According to Higgins, he was broke. Maybe he wasn't as broke as he let on. Longarm thought about looking in on the good doctor, but decided against it. Doctor Peabody was a mystery, and he might turn out to be the wrong kind of mystery, but Longarm was content to wait and see how the cards fell out.

They had ham steaks and mashed potatoes and redeye gravy and canned string beans for lunch. There were also corn dodgers and fresh butter. When Longarm commented on the pleasure of the butter, Mrs. Higgins said, "Laws, that reminds me. I got a churn full of milk clabbering. I don't get to churning, it will go sour just sure as shooting."

Rita Ann said, "I'll be glad to do it, Mrs. Higgins."

Mrs. Higgins patted her arm with her plump hand. "Bless you, girl, you are going to spoil me rotten."

Longarm gave her a look just as he was about to take a bite of cornbread. "Yeah, Rita Ann, you are just so sweet sugar wouldn't melt in your mouth."

She cocked her head and gave him a crooked little smile. "You should know, Mister Long, being my employer."

"I wish you'd keep reminding both of us about that. One of us seems to have a tendency to forget."

"Good vittles, Mrs. Higgins," Higgins said.

Longarm watched the thin man shovel down the food, and said, "Herman, I don't know where it all goes. I've seen you put away them groceries now for three meals, but I ain't seen none of it show."

"He's a fidget," Mrs. Higgins announced. "Just fidgets night and day. Commences fidgeting in the mornin' an' don't let up till he's snorin'."

Higgins gave her a dark look. "You'd fidget too if you had the weight on your shoulders I got on mine. Never can tell what might be about to happen round here."

Longarm cleared his throat and gave him a hard look. Higgins dropped his head and looked guilty. He said, "Canned beans is all right, but I'll be glad of spring and be able to get the real thing."

After lunch Longarm caught Rita Ann by the arm and walked her out the front door before she could disappear into the back with Mrs. Higgins. She put her hand over her eyes against the sun. "It's too hot," she said.

"Not as hot as some other things I know."

She gave him an innocent look. "Why, whatever are you talking about, Mr. Long?"

"Brushing my teeth."

"Didn't you get your teeth washed this morning?"

"Well, yeah, once I got my strength back. But it seemed like I had a little interference there for a few moments."

They had stopped a few yards from the front of the station. She said, "Didn't you like it?"

In spite of himself he blushed slightly. "Well, of course I liked it. Any man who wouldn't like that would have to be dead from the waist down. But look here, what makes you slip up on a man like that?"

She shrugged. "I just like what I like when I want it."

"I don't even know your last name."

She gave him an impish look. "Would that make it better if you did? Would you be able to say, 'Oh, Miss Smith, that's wonderful.' " She said it in a high falsetto and laughed.

"Damn you, girl," he swore. "You are the beatenest woman I ever run into. Have you given any thought to what you're going to do when you get to Phoenix? You'll still be in the same fix."

She cocked her head and eyed him. "You gave me to understand that I had a job with you. How come I won't have a job of employment in Phoenix as well as here? And where is all them things I'm supposed to be writing down?"

He shifted uncomfortably. "Well of course you've got a job with me. The only thing is, I got to take off for some rough country in New Mexico. Look at a ranch out there."

"Well, where are your headquarters? Can't I go there and wait? Do whatever work I'm supposed to do? Ain't they in Phoenix? Big cattleman like you ought to have a headquarters in a going town like Phoenix."

"I thought you didn't believe I was a cattleman."

"I don't, but as long as you want to say it, it's my job to agree with you. Isn't that my job, to be agreeable?"

He cleared his throat, feeling awkward. "Truth be," he said, "my headquarters are up in Colorado. In Denver."

"I bet it's nice there. Think I would like it?"

He looked away. "Oh, hell, Rita Ann, now you are teasing me."

"No, I'm just trying to get you to say that the money you gave me was a handout. Wasn't it? You didn't think I'd take it if you didn't make up some cock-and-bull story about a job."

He swerved his head back to her, stung. He said with heat in his voice, "Let's just wait and see, missy, whether there's a job or not." He dug down in his jeans and came out with his roll. He peeled off a twenty-dollar bill and tried to put it in her hand.

She put her arms behind her back. "I don't need any more money. And I didn't do what I did for money. I did it because I liked it and because I wanted to."

"'You are going to take this," he said. The scooped top of her blouse was slightly open. Before she could react he shoved the bill down inside. Then he stepped back. "Just like you, I did that because I like to and because I want to. You can't just have it your way."

She studied him through slitted eyes for a second, and then she stepped up close to him. She put her hand on his cheek and stretched up and kissed him softly on the lips. She left her hand there for a second. "You're a sweet man." Then she dropped her hand, turned on her heels, and walked back into the station.

He said, "Hey, wait a minute! I still don't know your last name."

Over her shoulder she said, "I have to go churn now. I'll tell you some other time."

Longarm stared after her, biting his lip. Somewhere, somehow, sometime, a broken, woebegone, timid little woman in a dowdy gray dress had gotten a hand up on him. He didn't know the how or the why of it, but he was damned if he was going to let the situation continue. When he danced, he liked to be the one doing the leading, even if he wasn't certain what the tune was.

It was late afternoon. Longarm was sitting in the Higginses's front room reading a week-old newspaper when he heard talking from the common room. It was men's voices, several of them. He recognized Mister Higgins's high-pitched gabble, but the others were strange. He wondered if the doctor had come in to try and cadge some real whiskey, but there was more than one strange voice and he knew it couldn't be the Mexicans. He got up from the easy chair he'd been sitting in and walked over to the door that opened on the common room. He peeked through the little slit that the door made where it was hinged to the wall. It wasn't much of a view, but the men were moving around and, one by one, they came into view.

They didn't appear to be anybody special, just three rough-looking characters who'd come in out of the sun. Higgins was behind the bar, pouring out whiskey for them. Longarm strained to get a sight of any of their gun rigs. One turned in just the right way, and Longarm could see that he was wearing a cutaway holster and a well-cared-for large-caliber revolver. But the thing that caught his attention was that the man had a tiedown on his holster. A tiedown was a little leather thong attached to the outside of the holster. A man could pull it up and loop it over the butt of his revolver to keep the gun from jostling out when he was riding in rough country or doing anything else that might cause the gun to fall out. A cutaway holster did not envelop much of the revolver, just the barrel and about halfway up the cylinders. It was made that way to facilitate getting the gun into play as quickly as possible. Men who did business with revolvers wore cutaway holsters, and men who did business with guns in which they were constantly on the move and had to be ready for anything, wore tiedowns on their cutaway holsters. These were not ordinary cowhands or workingmen passing through. A cowhand wore a holster that nearly swallowed his pistol. Since he seldom needed it, other than to shoot an occasional rattlesnake or drop the lead steer in a stampede, he was more concerned with not losing it. But these men did not want to lose an instant in the use of their weapons.

Longarm could feel little warning signals going off in his head. What were three gunmen—and that's what they appeared to be—doing showing up at a relay station in the middle of nowhere? A relay station that might be passing along a half-a-million-dollar bullion shipment? And with Carl Lowe just escaped from prison? Longarm did not like the way matters were shaping up at all.

He wanted a look at their horses. He wanted to see if he could tell how far they had come, what quality animals they were, and if the men were leading pack animals. But there was no way out of the Higginses' living quarters except through the door he was at, and he did not want the men to get a look at him, not just yet. He turned and went into the back where Mrs. Higgins and Rita Ann were taking turns working at the churn. He got Mrs. Higgins's attention and motioned her to follow him. He led her into the front room with her wearing a worried look. "Is something gone amiss, Mar—Mr. Long?"

He said, "Sylvia, there are some men out at the bar drinking whiskey. I need to speak to Herman, but I don't want the men to know I'm here. I want you to go out and, just as casual as you can, tell Herman you need him in the back for a moment. Can you do that?"

Her eyes got round and she began to look nervous. "Why, why, why, I reckon I can. Is we fixin' to be held up? Robbed? Murdered?"

He shook his head. "No, no, Sylvia. Nothing like that. This is just ordinary peace-officer work. But I need to speak to Herman without anyone being the wiser. And

I don't see no use in you telling Rita Ann about this little errand.''

She hesitated, wiping her hands on her apron. "Just tell him I need to see him back here?''

"Yes. Something about the churn. Tell him it will only take a moment.''

She sighed, looking as if she were being sent on a dangerous mission. "Well, I'll shore try.''

He watched as she slipped through the door and then went up to the bar and tapped her husband on the shoulder. For a moment he frowned and shook his head, but then she folded her arms and gave him a look and he began to nod. Longarm saw him say something to the three men, then come around the bar end and follow his wife toward the door.

Chapter 5

Higgins came through the door intent on following his wife. Longarm grabbed his arm as he passed and then put a finger to his lips. He stepped over and shut the door to the common room, and then crossed to the door to the Higginses' bedroom and shut that door. Higgins was staring at him, mystified. Longarm said, "Who are those men out there?"

Higgins shrugged. "Jus' some fellers ridin' through, I reckon."

"Never saw them before?"

Higgins shook his head. "Not that I recollect."

"You get many strangers passing through here like that?"

Higgins scratched his head and frowned. "Is this law work? Is this serious bid'ness?"

"It could be. Did you get a look at their horses?"

"I seen 'em when they rode up. Plain ol' horses, near as I can figure. Didn't look stolen if that be what you mean. Though I wouldn't know how to tell a stolen horse. I was standin' out front so I seen 'em from a patch away."

"Which way were they coming from?"

Higgins frowned in concentration. "I'd say more from

84

the west, though it be hard to say. They is some bad ground due south of here, so they might have swung around that.''

''They have any pack animals with them?''

''No, now that you mention it, they didn't.'' Higgins scratched his head harder. ''Which is a strange thing. Most folks don't get off in this country without a pack animal totin' some extra water and vittles.''

''You never answered when I asked you if you get many strangers passing through here.''

Higgins stared at the door to the common room as if there might be an answer there. ''Wa'l, now and again, from time to time, different folks who have had bid'ness down south at the mines come north by this route. Generally the miners take the stage, but now and again a sportin' genn'lman or a drummer hawkin' some gadget or a cowhand will come this way, riding from station to station.'' He stared at the door again. ''Come to think of it, that do be a little strange, three hombres jus' showin' up like that out of nowhere. Wonder who in hell they *are*?''

''What'd they want?''

Higgins was looking more and more concerned. ''Wa'l, first thing they wanted a drink of whiskey, an' then they wanted to know if I had any beds. When I said no, they wondered if they could spread they bedrolls in the lee of the buildin' in case a wind come up. Said they'd like to make a fahr and would be glad to pay for the wood 'cause they knowed it must come pretty dear in a place like this.''

''Didn't ask to eat?''

''Yeah, they done that.'' Higgins nodded. ''I tol' 'em my old woman could fix them some grits and beans and maybe a pan of cornbread. Nothin' fancy. They said that would be fine.'' Higgins glanced at the door again. ''Seem like mighty nice fellers. Maybe they ain't nothin' wrong with them at all.''

Longarm turned and looked as if he too thought studying the door might tell him something. But then he

85

shook his head. "Herman, I can't have them hanging around the station, not with that stage due tomorrow."

"You reckon it might be a bullion run?" Higgins's eyes got big.

"I don't know. And neither do you. But there appear to be a few too many coincidences happening around here. Did their horses look hard-used?"

Higgins thought. "Wa'l, fact of the bid'ness is I can't say. Didn't notice. Want me to go take a look?"

"No. But they want to overnight here?"

"That's what they sayin'."

"And going to travel in the heat of the day tomorrow. Don't that strike you strange?"

"Wa'l, yessir, now that you mention it. How we goin' to get rid of 'em? You want me to go out there and tell 'em to clear off?"

Longarm shook his head. "No. You don't have any reason." He unbuckled his gunbelt and walked over and laid it on the divan. He had been thinking of how to approach the situation. "At least you don't have a reason right now. But I'm going to give you one."

"What would that be?"

Longarm unbuttoned the cuffs of his shirt and started rolling up his sleeves. "I'm going to go out there and start a fight with them. Do you have a shotgun?"

"Course. Place like this you'd always have a shotgun. Double-barreled, twelve-gauge. How come you took yore gunbelt off, Marshal?"

"Because I got good reason to think those hombres are gunmen. They wear their revolvers like *pistoleros*. I hate to do it, but I'm going to get into a fistfight. And I ain't been in a fistfight in a hell of a long time, but I don't want guns getting into it. It could be they are innocent of anything except stealing jam, and I don't want to kill one for nothing."

Higgins was starting to look nervous but excited. "What'll you be wanting me to do?"

Longarm said, "Well, there are three of them. One is pretty small and the other is a little pudgy, but there is one my size and maybe a few good years younger. I can't whip all three, but I can start a ruckus. Soon as I get things going you come running out with your scattergun and go to yelling for us to cease and desist.'' He saw the confused look on Higgins's face. ''Go to yelling for us to quit it, to stop. Say there ain't no fighting allowed in the place and that I am your employee and you ain't going to stand for them beating up on me. Shoot a barrel into the wall or the ceiling if you have to. I just don't want to have all three of them stomping on me.''

Higgins licked his lips. ''Wha-what do I do if they, if one of them draws a gun or somethin'?''

''They won't, but don't worry about it. If one does, I'll handle it. Now, you got all this?''

''Got everything except my shotgun. It be back in the bedroom.''

''Well, get it, but don't say nothing. You understand?''

''Why, my stars and garters, Marshal, you reckon I'm crazy? If Sylvie knew what I was about to do she'd have a fit.''

Longarm waited until the stationkeeper had gone into the back and returned carrying the big-bore shotgun over his arm. He had it broken open, and Longarm could see the brass ends of the two big shells. Longarm motioned for Higgins to shut the door behind him. When he'd done so, Longarm said, ''You attract any attention?''

Higgins shook his head. ''They was busy fillin' up butter molds. Guess the churnin' is all done. How you figure to get after 'em, Marshal?''

Longarm said grimly, ''I'll think of something. Starting a fight is a hell of a lot easier than stopping one. Remember that I'm your employee and when things get calmed down, you tell them they will have to move on. No matter what they say or offer, you make it clear they'd better get on down the road.''

Higgins looked worried. ''Them is some mighty rough-lookin' folks, Marshal. You said one was little and one was pudgy, but they didn't look all that much like that to me. You ain't fixin' to get yoreself in no storm, be you?''

Longarm smiled. "I hope not, Herman. I certainly hope not. But it won't be the first time. I'm going to close this door behind me, but you stand ready to come through when you hear it getting rowdy. And don't be bashful about raising your voice. I hate to scrap around on the floor like some schoolkid, but I don't know any other way."

"Why don't you jus' take this here musket and run 'em off?"

Longarm looked at him. "If they are who I think they are, that will just put them on their guard. No. I want this to seem like it has nothing to do with what I think they are up to." He reached up to make sure the pocket where he carried his badge was buttoned. He didn't want that falling out in the middle of the fight.

Finally he went over and took hold of the knob and turned it. He dreaded how his face and fists were going to feel in a very short time. Even when you won you always got hurt some in a fistfight.

He stepped into the common room. The three men were standing at the plank bar drinking whiskey. They looked up as he slammed the door behind him. The one nearest to him was the smaller man. He had thin features and was wearing a flat-brimmed, flat-crowned tan hat. He looked clean-shaven, but then he didn't look old enough where shaving had become a problem. It was the next man that took Longarm's eye. He was at least thirty, with heavy shoulders and big arms. He had a round, hard-looking face with deep-set, small eyes set back under his eyebrows. The third man Longarm couldn't see very well because he was blocked by the bigger man in the middle. But Longarm did, quickly, see that all three were wearing cutaway holsters with tiedowns over the butts of their revolvers.

It was only a few paces to the bar. He took them in quick strides. The men were watching him, glasses in their hands. He said in a hard voice, "You boys have made a mistake. Ain't no whiskey for sale here. That whiskey is my private stock."

It was the big man who turned slightly to face him. He said in a casual voice, "Likely you are wrong there, feller. We bought these here drinks from the station-keeper. Not five minutes ago. So if it be yore private goods, he don't know it."

Longarm had edged up until he was only about two feet from the smaller man. But it was not him that he intended to take out of the fight first. The first punch was going to be the important one, and he intended that for the big man with the big shoulders.

Longarm took a small step to his left to bring the man into range. He said, talking over the head of the smaller man, "That old man don't run this place, I do. An' I'm tellin' you that ain't whiskey for sale. We don't take no saddle trash in here and won't be no grub neither. Now drink down what you got and get out the door."

The big man pushed himself away from the bar. He said over his shoulder to the pudgy man Longarm couldn't quite see, "Frank, looks like we got us some homegrown meanness right here. He gonna run us off. Done called us saddle trash. What you think of that?"

Longarm edged further to his left to bring the man who had been called Frank into view. But he didn't want to see Frank; he wanted to see Frank's side arm and where it was. It was still in the holster and the tiedown was still over the butt, but Frank's hand was dangerously close to a position to change all that in the bat of an eye. Longarm said, "He better think it's a good idea 'cause I am fixin' to start throwing you snakes out of here in just about five seconds."

The big man had his weight on both his feet. His little pig eyes were watching Longarm with delight. He looked like a man who was about to have some fun. He said, "You hear that, Frank? He called us snakes and said he was gonna throw us all in the sand in about five seconds. All of us. That right, feller?"

Longarm said, "Don't be calling me any of your family names, *feller*. Now turn around and walk toward that door."

The big man laughed slightly and turned his head toward the man behind him. As he did Longarm raised his right hand as if to scratch his ear. But he only got his hand just above shoulder height. There it suddenly turned into a fist and he drove off his right foot, stepping forward with his left, putting his whole shoulder behind the punch. The blow hit the big man flush in the face just as he was turning to face Longarm again. Longarm saw his fist hit the man on the upper lip and the lower part of his nose. He saw blood fly, and felt something crunch beneath his knuckles. It was either teeth or the bone in the man's nose.

The big man went over backwards, falling into the pudgy man behind him. But Longarm didn't wait to see the results. The stride of the punch had taken him even with the small man and he pivoted on the balls of his feet, pulling his right boot back, and then hit the smaller man with a sweeping left on the side of the head. The man's hat flew off and his face banged down on the planks of the bar. As he bounced up Longarm had already drawn his right hand back, and he caught the man under the chin as he was trying to rise. It was more of an uppercut than anything, and it lifted the man off the floor and leaned him partly over the bar before he slid down to the floor.

But even while he was hitting the smaller man Longarm was already moving down the bar to where the pudgy man was trying to scramble up. Longarm saw that he was trying to jerk loose the tiedown on his revolver. With a swift move Longarm kicked out with his right foot, catching the man on the hand with the heel of his boot. The pudgy man yelled and fell back. But by now, his face smeared with blood, the first man was trying to struggle to his feet. Longarm quickly shifted his weight and kicked the first man under the chin with the toe of his left boot. The man made a groan and rolled over on his back, knocking over one of the wooden stools. Longarm took a quick glance behind him, saw that the smaller man was still on the floor and too groggy to be a danger, and whirled and went over the outstretched form of the big man with the bloody nose, diving more than stepping, and hit the pudgy man as hard as he could in the stomach with his right fist. The man instantly doubled up and sat down. It took a half second to get his feet under him, but when he could, Longarm swung from the floor and hit the man under the chin and knocked him over on his back. At that instant he became aware of an outcry behind him. He turned.

"HOLD IT! HOLD IT! QUIT THAT FIGHTIN'! I WON'T HAVE NO FIGHTIN' IN HERE! YOU ARE SCARIN' THE WIMMEN!"

Higgins looked wild, his hair touseled and his shirt out, holding the big shotgun almost at the ready. He was yelling at the top of his voice. "CUT OUT THIS QUARRELIN'! AIN'T NO FIGHTIN' IN HERE! BY DAMN I'LL LET THIS CANNON OFF THE BUNCH OF YOU DON'T SETTLE DOWN! AND I MEAN RIGHT NOW!"

Longarm watched him with mild amusement. The smaller man was not even conscious yet. The pudgy gunman was sitting up, holding his stomach and looking sick. The man with the heavy shoulders had propped himself up on one arm and was feeling his nose with the hand of the other. There was no fight to be stopped.

Longarm said heavily, "Herman, I'm damn glad you come out here. They was stealin' whiskey and fixin' to whip me in the bargain. Keep that shotgun on 'em. They is a dangerous lot." He didn't know if he sounded dumb enough to be someone working at a relay station, but he was enjoying the lying.

Higgins stepped closer, aiming the shotgun down at the men on the floor and sweeping it back and forth. He said in an outraged voice, "By golly, so that's how you'll have it! Why, damn it to hell, I ought to let this here blunderbuss off an' blow the lot of you to Hell!'' He looked up at Longarm. "Stealin' whiskey, was they?"

Longarm nodded. "Yessir, they was. An' threatenin' me with their pistols. I was scairt for my very life.''

From the floor the man with the big shoulders straightened up. He spat out a mouthful of blood and said thoughtfully, "I think that sonofabitch broke my nose.''

Longarm pointed at him. "See how he is cussin' me, Herman. How come you let such saddle trash in?"

Higgins shook his head sorrowfully. Longarm could see he was really getting into the part he was playing. "I'll tell you, this is what comes of tryin' to do yore feller man a favor. They wanted to shade up an' I let 'em. Wanted whiskey an' I give it to 'em. Wanted to water their horses and I said shore. An' now look what come of it. Onliest man I've ever had would stay out here and work, an' they take guns to you and go to beaten' on yore head! Damn my socks! Ain't I ever gonna learn?"

The one who had been called Frank let go of his stomach long enough to help himself to his feet by leaning on the overturned stool. He said, gritting his teeth, "Old man, look round you. Who done the whippin' up? You see any blood on yore damned hired hand? You see a lump on him? Is he down on the floor with blood on his face?"

Higgins waved the shotgun at him. "You better not fool with me, boy! You've abused my hospitality all I'm gonna stand fer! Dammit, you don't know how to act civilized, you can clear out of here and right now!"

Frank said to the man who'd thought his nose was broken, "Wayne, the old man wants us to leave. What do you reckon?"

Wayne was trying to get up, holding on to the bar. He said, "I heard him, Frank." He stared at Longarm.

"For a hay forker he fights pretty good." Then he shifted to Higgins. "We paid for that whiskey. You taken our money."

Longarm was watching all three. The smaller one was shaking his head and groaning, not fully conscious. But Longarm didn't like the way Frank and Wayne had their hands too near their revolvers. He suddenly reached out and took the shotgun from Mister Higgins. He took a quick look to make sure the safety wasn't on and then said, "By damn, don't you come round here blackening my name! I got to live here. I saw ya'll sneakin' whiskey an' ain't no use you denyin' it. Now the bunch of you can gather up yore traps an' get on out of here! I'm tired of foolin' with you and this shotgun just might go off by itself!"

Higgins said warningly, "Don't fool with him, boys! Don't fool with him! Got a temper on him like a team of mules! Don't work him up, now, don't work him up. I can't answer fer it. He's got the shotgun. It's in his hands. Heaven only knows what might happen now!"

The one called Wayne, keeping his eyes on the shotgun in Longarm's hands, reached down for the small man, who was still on the floor. He got him by the upper arm and lifted him easily to his feet. He said, "Get up, Potts. We ain't wanted here. Man holdin' a shotgun on us. Get yore head cleared."

Behind him Frank, still holding his belly, said to Longarm, "What'd you start this fight for, feller? We wadn't doin' you no harm."

Longarm gave him a thin smile, but kept to the demeanor of a stablehand. "I never started no fight, *feller*. You three was makin' mighty free with my whiskey. We don't get that stuff in here ever' day. I told Herman here"—he jerked his head toward Higgins—"that the day this place run out of whiskey was the day I went walkin' out of here. Ain't that right, Herman."

Higgins stepped forward. He said earnestly, "Oh, my, yeah! Laws, I never thought. We was runnin' low an' I never thought, not bein' partial to the stuff myself, but Bull here won't be caught short without it.''

Wayne eyed Longarm. ''Bull, huh? Well, Bull, we'll get out. But they will come another day.''

Longarm lifted the shotgun menacingly. ''You better hope for yore sake that day don't come. You gettin' off light as is and it's only cause of Herman here. Now pick up what you've dropped and git outten here!''

Higgins said placatingly, ''Now, Bull, you done whipped 'em. Don't be kickin' 'em when they are down.''

''They mouthed me, Herman. They mouthed me. An' you know I don't stand fer no mouthin'. They went to joshin' me like I was some hick. You know I don't take to that.''

Higgins looked at them sorrowfully. ''I'm right sorry to hear 'bout that. Bull ain't the man to rag 'bout his country ways. Nossir! Best not to do it.''

They were all up now, standing in a line with their back to the front door. Wayne said, a little blood still running out of his nose, ''He don't fight like no hayseed.'' He narrowed his little eyes sunk deep in their sockets. ''He fights like somebody seen a good many saloon brawls. He knew who to throw the first punch at.''

Longarm did not care for the way Wayne was talking. It meant his little act was not going over as successfully as he wanted. He said, motioning with the shotgun, ''You just put some money on the bar fer them last drinks that ya'll taken while Herman was outten the room. I seen you through the door. You can't put one over on me. Now, you better let me hear that silver ring.''

Potts was the one closest to the bar. Wayne said, ''Put a couple of dollars down, Potts. Turns out the man is going to rob us in the bargain.''

Longarm drew both hammers back on the big shotgun and raised it to his shoulder. ''I reckon that mouth you are talking out of ain't doing too good a job. What say I make you one in yore belly."

Higgins said, "Now, Bull. Now, Bull. Take it easy."

But then Potts dug in his pocket and pitched two silver dollars on the bar. He said, "We never taken no second drink, but there's money anyway."

Longarm said, "Now, you *fellers,* as you like to call other folks who don't care to be called that, ya'll get to marchin' backwards out that door. Step along now."

He followed them stride for stride as they backed toward the front door. Wayne said, "We leave you enough whiskey? You reckon what's left will handle you till supplies can arrive?"

Longarm said, "Git!"

Frank said, "For a mule hustler you seem mighty at home with that scattergun."

"It's a rabbit-getter. But you three be a bunch bigger than a rabbit. Stay bunched up now, on account of I ain't got but the two barrels and I'd have to get a brace of you with one shot. And I wouldn't let a single finger get near them fancy shootin' irons of yores. Make sure none of them little leather strings falls off the handles neither."

They were at the door. Frank said, "Now what?"

Longarm was keeping about two yards between them. He said, "Now you rush out there and get on yore horses and see how fast you can get out of shotgun range. But by that time I'll have a carbine in my hand so I'd keep on goin' was I you."

"You just a regular Jesse James, ain't you."

"Move! Now! NOW!"

They went through the door in a bunch. Longarm ran up to the wall and peeked around the opening. He could see them getting to their horses and mounting. One started to pull his carbine out of the saddle boot, but Longarm stuck the barrel of the shotgun around the door. They turned their horses and spurred away, heading north. As they rode, Wayne yelled back, "I ain't forgetting this, hayseed. That other day is coming!"

Longarm turned in time to see the laugh building in Higgins. He clamped his hand over the old man's mouth and indicated he should be quiet. He nodded his head toward their private quarters. Higgins bobbed his head that he understood, and Longarm took his hand away. Higgins immediately giggled, though in a low tone. He said gravely, "Well, Bull, I reckon we handled them *hombres*." Then he couldn't help himself. He slapped his knee and let out a chortle. "Boy, howdy, that was plumb fun! Is law work allus this much fun? Hot damn! I got to tell Sylvie 'bout this. She'll have a fit. We shore fooled them, huh, Bull? Heh, heh, heh."

Longarm rubbed his jaw thoughtfully. "I don't know, Herman. That one was mighty suspicious. I don't know if my acting like a stable hand fooled him. I did too good in the fight. Stable hands ain't supposed to know how to fight like that."

Higgins's eyes got round. He said, "Boy, I'll say you done good in the fight. Last thing I saw move that fast was my ol' woman when she spilt a big pot of bilin' grits on the floor and her in her bare feet. You whupped up on them some mighty good. And say, I thought we done pretty good way we played our parts."

Longarm shrugged. "Herman, those men are up to something. I don't know what it is, but they make me uneasy. They are not strangers passing through. We didn't run off innocent men. Those are paid gunmen or I'm a Hoosier. And I never set foot in that state in my life. I don't think I fooled them."

"Well, you fooled me. Lordy, I got so carried 'way watchin' you knockin' 'em around I nearly forgot my part."

Longarm looked around at him and half smiled. "I was beginning to wonder. Lucky for me I got that biggest one out of the way before he could even matters out."

"You shore fetched him a lick! Went down like a poled steer. Wait'll I tell Sylvie 'bout this!"

Longarm suddenly frowned. "Listen, Herman, until

I'm sure about what the hell is going on, I don't reckon we ought to be telling anyone anything. When it comes to explaining this to the ladies, I reckon you better leave it up to me.''

Higgins looked slightly crestfallen. He said, ''Shore, if that be the way you want it. But you won't tell it like I seen it. Or how me an' you done that actin' like we was on the stage or somethin'. What'd you think of me comin' up with that name? Bull. What'd you think of that?''

Longarm looked at him and said dryly, ''What's my last name? Shit?''

Higgins giggled. ''See? You won't put all the good parts in. Can't I just tell Sylvie about it tonight after we be in bed?''

Longarm shook his head. ''You can tell her after we are gone on the stage tomorrow.'' He glanced at the door, noting that it was ajar. ''I think our birds are already flitting around. Remember, you leave the telling to me.'' He raised his voice and called, ''Ladies? Ladies? Rough stuff is over. You can come out now.''

They came through the door with Mrs. Higgins in the lead. They looked around. Other than the two overturned stools there wasn't much to see. Mrs. Higgins fixed her husband with a look. ''Mr. Higgins, I'd be obliged to know what has been going on in this place that required you to run for a shotgun.'' She looked at Longarm, who was holding the weapon. He hastily set it on the floor and leaned it against the bar as if to distance himself from it. ''Has this place become unsafe for civilized folks?'' Mrs. Higgins asked.

Longarm said quickly, ''Just some riders that got out of hand. Maybe had too much whiskey in them. Not a lot happened, Sylvia. And you get to be right proud of your husband. He set them straight about behavior around here and made it mighty clear.''

Rita Ann walked across the floor and looked at several red splotches on the floor where the man with the nosebleed had spit. She said, "Looks like somebody cut his finger on something."

Longarm was trying to hide his hands, which he knew were skinned and bruised. They'd swell up if he didn't get to soaking them fairly soon. He said, "Well, I figured to maybe help ease them out. I didn't want to see no gunshots getting fired. One of 'em must have scuffed his knee or his hand or something."

Mrs. Higgins sniffed. "Sounded to us like was a herd of cattle runnin' loose through the place." She rounded on her husband. "Then I hear this one yelling at the top of his lungs about blowing people in half. Laws! Nearly scared me and Rita Ann to death. We never knowed from one second to the other what to think. And couldn't see much through the crack in the door."

Higgins said placatingly, "Now, Sylvie, we git them kind through here now and again. We's jus' lucky we had Mister Long here to help out with matters. They was only some bullies needed showing the error of their ways. And we done that, didn't we, Mr. Long."

"Yes, yes, Herman. We sure did. You did the biggest part of it, of course. But I thought you handled the situation right nicely. You ought to be proud, Mrs. Higgins, Sylvia. Quite a man, your husband."

Mrs. Higgins gave him a stern look and said, "He ain't big as a minute and thinks he can take on the world. One of these days he is gonna bite off more than he can chew and then we'll just have to see about it." But at the tail end of her look, a little maternal fondness came into the sternness. "I guess I'll keep him."

Rita Ann came over to Longarm and before he could react, took his right hand in hers and lifted it up. The scuffs across the knuckle were clear. She dropped it and picked up the left. It had a cut across the first two knuckles. She said, "Looked like it must have been a two-fisted fight. Didn't go exactly the way you told it, Mr. Long."

He cleared his throat. "Well, there was a little scuffling. But not enough to write home about. However, I

98

would be obliged to get a pan of warm salty water and maybe soak these here mitts of mine before they get sore.''

Mrs. Higgins said, ''I'd be obliged. You jus' give me a minute to run into the kitchen and I'll fetch it right out here. Herman, you come along with me. You ain't out of the woods about this scuffling affair. No, sir. Not by a long shot. I'll have a few more words with you, mister.''

Higgins said, ''Now there you go, Sylvie, makin' a cow outten a kitten. They ain't nothin' else to it.''

But he followed her obediently as she walked back into their living quarters.

As soon as they were out of sight Longarm turned immediately and started for the front door. He wanted to make sure the three men had kept riding and had not cut around to approach them from the back. He was aware that Rita Ann was following him, but he walked 50 yards out in front of the relay station and slowly swept his eyes across the terrain from north to south to east to west and then back north again. He could just pick out some little dots moving along at a pretty good pace. They appeared to be about three or four miles away. It could be the three that had come in the station, or it could be three entirely different men. He meant to speak to Higgins as soon as he conveniently could about putting his Mexicans on watch. It wouldn't hurt to keep a close lookout until dusk.

Behind him Rita Ann said, ''Why did you beat those three men up?''

He whirled around. ''What?''

She said, ''I could see a little through the crack between the door and the wall. It was almost over by the time we got there, but I saw that two men were laying on the floor and I saw you kick one in the head when he tried to get up. Why'd you do that?''

He stared at her. ''Hell, Mr. Higgins told you. They were making trouble. They started in on him and I had to step in and help.''

She shook her head. "No, that is not true. Mr. Higgins was back getting the shotgun when the trouble started. I heard it. You were the one out there. You were the one using your fists. I saw you had left your gunbelt on the divan, which means you had gone out there to fight. You didn't want to be weighed down by it."

He gave her a perplexed look. "Who the hell are you? The sheriff? I don't know exactly how it happened, but Mr. Higgins came back through the door and said it looked like he was going to have to run some hombres off, so I went out to see what was going on. I didn't wear my gunbelt because I didn't want to take a chance on any shooting. Damn! Talk about minding other folks' business! What the hell has this got to do with you?"

"Nothing," she said calmly. "I only want to know who you are."

"I've told you. How many times I got to tell you?"

"You're a businessman. Well, from the way you fight I'd recommend you go in the fighting business."

He said, "I always wondered who the person would be who exasperated me beyond my reason. I think I may be looking at her." Then he stepped around her and went back into the station, where Mrs. Higgins was waiting with the pan of hot, salty water.

Supper that night was a subdued affair. Higgins said, "You know, I'm gonna be right sorry, Mr. Long, to see you and Miss Rita Ann leave on that stage tomorrow. Place won't be the same, will it, Sylvie?"

She said, "I should think not. I know I've enjoyed the company of another woman. Especially one as bright and gay as Rita Ann." She sighed. "But then all good things must come to an end. That's what my dear old mother said."

Longarm looked at Rita Ann. "And bad ones too, I hope."

They had gotten to bed early that night, not much after ten. Longarm had turned into his blankets naked, in anticipation of Rita Ann's arrival. Part of him was aroused, but part of him was also angry. She had called the turn at every juncture. If she came to him this night it was going to be different.

She was so long in coming that he was almost asleep when he realized she was standing by him in the voluminous nightgown she had borrowed from Mrs. Higgins. He sat up immediately as she began to pull the gown over her head. When it fell to the floor she stood there, again reflected in the firelight, while he studied her beautiful body with true appreciation. Then she slowly knelt down, landing on her knees on the edge of his blankets. She was about to reach for him when he took her under the shoulders and lifted her onto his bed on her back. Then, moving too fast for her to realize what he was doing, he was on top of her, prying her legs apart. He fell forward, guiding himself into her and covering her mouth with his at the same time. He held her by the buttocks, one in each hand, and began pulling her into him, making her rhythm match his. He started slowly, but then he began thrusting harder and harder, almost angrily. As he probed her depths he could feel her gasping out of the corners of her mouth, but he wouldn't let her mouth loose from his. Her hips were starting to arch up, clearing the blanket by six inches. She hoisted her legs and wrapped them around his middle, squeezing him tight. They were locked in an intertwined and frenzied embrace. He kept thrusting and thrusting, pushing her up the blankets.

She began to tremble, and then she began to shake. He poured more savagery into the rhythm of his plunging, speeding it up, filling her, forcing himself deep inside her. She was gasping now, trembling and shaking and clawing at his back.

Then, suddenly, he could hear her yelling inside his mouth. Her screaming went on for a long, long time, kept silent within his own cheeks and lips, as her heels drummed on his back and her nails raked his neck and shoulders.

As suddenly as it had started it ended. She went limp.

Her arms slid from around his neck and fell to the blankets. Her legs came off his back and fell down beside his. He took his mouth away and she lay there, her eyes open, her mouth gasping, staring straight up. Very slowly he eased off her, easing off on the side toward the wall. He pulled the blanket up around his shoulder. He said softly in her ear, "Good night."

She turned her face and looked at him. "What?"

"I said good night."

She sighed. "I don't think I can move." Then she turned her head back to him. "What about you?"

"I'm fine," he said. "I just wanted you to understand there was more than one unselfish person in this bed."

Chapter 6

The stage arrived a little before three o'clock the next day. They'd been watching for it for a half an hour, and then it topped a little rise a mile away and was suddenly on them. Higgins and the two Mexicans went out into the stable yard to help the driver stop the team. Longarm could see from his vantage point that the mules were worked up and sweating. There were five span of them, ten mules, and the driver handled the double handful of reins with practiced ease. To his left the shotgun messenger, as such men were called, held on to the side of his high seat and waved as they arrived.

Longarm watched as the two Mexicans ran alongside the lead mules, catching them by the harness and turning them in an arc, bending them back so that they began to circle. The driver was standing up in his seat, his hands full of reins, pulling with all his might. But the mules were run out, and after one circle of the yard, they pulled up in front of the station and stopped.

The stage was empty. Longarm walked over and looked at it curiously. It was the same shape as a buckboard except considerably bigger. He reckoned it to be about five feet wide by ten or twelve feet long. It had big, steel-rimmed wheels that were at least six inches wide, the better to ride over the sandy dirt. The stage had an almost flat canvas top and long canvas curtains that could be let down on both sides, presumably to keep out the rain, though more likely the dust and the sun. At the very front was a wooden box that was about three feet wide and ran the width of the bed of the stage. It was high enough so that it extended up behind the driver's seat and up to the canvas roof. Longarm figured he knew what was in the box, and he didn't reckon it was used clothes. The end he could see had a door in it with a heavy padlock holding a hasp. He could see that the box not only served its function to hold the safe, but also stuck up high enough to protect the driver and the guard from attack from the rear. And the passengers would have a hard time reaching their way up to the driver's box if they were of a mind to try. The box blocked their way, and there was nothing to hold on to while they tried to get at the driver or the guard.

He was a little surprised that the stage was empty, but Higgins told him that was the case more often than not. "Most of the traffic we get in people is when they let a bunch out at the mine or a new bunch is going down there or there's some boss or such taking a vacation. Of course we get passengers will take the stage to get somewhere along the line, but not all that often."

The driver's name was Ben, and his guard was a man that Higgins called Wooly. They were both old stage hands who, as they all did, said they wished they had a nickel for every drop of mule sweat they'd wiped off their faces. They were wind-burned and sun-cured and anxious for a drink. Ben said, "We got a little ahead of schedule. Reckon we'll shade up here a bit."

Longarm was ready to go. While the drivers rested he carried his saddle and saddlebags out to the coach. There was a rack on top of the stage that he figured was for luggage. He stepped up on the bed of the wagon at the end and slung his saddle into the rack along with his saddlebags. After a moment's thought he stepped up again, pulled his carbine out of the saddle boot, and looked into the interior of the coach. There were benches along each side with padded backs. He slid his rifle in under the left-hand one near the end. He figured it would be ready to hand from there. After that he went back into the station. Mrs. Higgins and Rita Ann were fussing over a cloth valise that Mrs. Higgins was insisting Rita Ann use to carry her new clothes. Her case had not come in on the stage and it appeared, Rita Ann said, that she'd have to make do with what Mrs. Higgins had given her until the stage company could find a way to get her case to her.

The biggest trouble was with Doctor Peabody. He was insisting that the stage owed him free passage back to Phoenix since they had thrown him off in the middle of nowhere. Higgins said heatedly, "We don't owe you nothin'. It was yore bad actin' got you throwed off that stage. Tryin' to look up the dresses of a bunch of hoors. So now it is three dollars on the barrel head or you can sit out thar an' an' drink with them Mexicans till they throw you out. Damned if I care."

The doctor whined that the stage was furnishing passage for the lady, Rita Ann, and their cases were similar.

"Not a bit of it!" Higgins said staunchly. "She was done wrong. *You* done wrong. They is a ocean full of difference 'tween them two."

In the end the doctor fumbled through the pockets of his soiled suit until he found three crumpled one-dollar bills. Higgins issued him a ticket and a stern warning to behave himself. "Else they is liable to throw you out in the big middle of nowhere an' you'll have buzzards fer company."

Longarm went back outside and watched the Mexicans putting the new team in place. They harnessed up the mules a span at a time, and they did it with a sureness and quickness he had to admire. Really, he thought, it took a good Mexican to work with Spanish mules. They seemed to have an understanding of the brutes that nobody else did. Finally the team was in the traces and ready to go. The mules that had just finished their run were in the corral, lathered up and still mixing around nervously, unable to settle down.

Finally it was time to go. Longarm hugged Mrs. Higgins and thanked her for all her help. He shook Higgins's hand and promised the old man he'd be hearing from him. He gave him a wink that no one else could see and said, "I'll see that you get all the news."

They climbed aboard. Rita Ann went in first, and she went all the way to the front and sat on the left-hand bench. The doctor went in and sat midway down on the right-hand side. Longarm sat at the tail end on the left, over his Winchester carbine.

Before he climbed up to his seat Ben, the driver, stuck his head in the coach to tell them he'd be taking it kind of slow at first. "That is," he said, "if I can hold these damn mules. They is a pretty good grade starts about ten miles this side of the next station, an' if I let these mules run right off they won't have a blame thing left to pull that grade. They is mules in this string that have made that very same mistake, but you can't learn a derned mule nothin'. So don't get fretty if it seems like we are pokin' along. We'll get there."

They pulled out at three-thirty under a hot afternoon sun. The stage jerked as the mules were let go by the Mexicans holding their heads. Longarm could feel the run in them, almost see the driver straining against the reins to hold them back. And at first, it didn't seem like he would be able. As Longarm leaned out and waved to Mr. and Mrs. Higgins the landscape was passing at an alarming rate. But gradually, the driver got control and brought the mules down to a slow trot. Longarm could hear him swearing over the crunch and swish of the iron-rimmed tires.

Longarm looked around. The doctor had his head on his chest, swaying with the motion of the coach, seeming to be catching a quick nap. Longarm looked down the bench at Rita Ann. She was half facing forward, looking out the side of the coach. She had had very little to say to him after the episode of the night before. Some moments after he'd said good night and closed his eyes, she had slipped away back to her bed on the divan. In the morning she had been as pleasant as she was supposed to be in front of the Higginses. There had been no opportunity for him to get her alone to talk and see how she liked having someone else call the tune. The doctor had come in a little before noon and had been given some lunch with them, and then there had been the business of packing and getting ready. Higgins had called him aside and held an earnest and long conversation about what help he could be if anything unlawful came up. So between one thing and another, Longarm and Rita Ann had not really spoken. He thought she was acting cool toward him, but then she always had been cool. Perhaps she didn't want to give him the satisfaction of acting like something unusual had happened. Well, he thought, she could just sit up in front of the stage and keep to herself. It made no difference to him. He was only grateful to finally be moving and somewhat on the trail of Carl Lowe. And then there was the matter of the three riders from the day before. He couldn't shake it out of his mind that they were somewhere up ahead, waiting. It didn't make any sense that three gunmen would be riding across the Arizona badlands with no purpose in mind, and he figured he was riding in a coach that contained a few hundred thousand purposes. He looked out the back of the coach and saw that the relay station had dropped below the horizon. In spite of the driver's best efforts, they were moving right along. But it was still going to be a long ride to Buckeye and the railroad and a serious effort to track Carl Lowe. He settled back, wishing he had a cigar. He had a bottle of whiskey, but that was in his saddlebags and his saddlebags were on top of the coach in the luggage rack.

They rode on, the heat really making itself felt now. The mules had been slowed down to a walk in anticipation of the pull up the grade that lay ahead. Longarm yawned and looked out his side. When he brought his eyes back into the coach the doctor was apparently awake. He smiled at Longarm. "Nice day, wouldn't you say, sir?"

Longarm yawned again. "Yeah, if we were under a shade tree. Could do with a little rain."

The doctor had his little black bag at his feet. He said, "I believe it is time for a light libation."

Longarm said, "That stuff will kill you in this heat."

The doctor said, "Not as fast as this." When he brought his hand out of the bag he was holding a large-caliber revolver. He said, "Wouldn't you agree that a bullet is faster than whiskey, Marshal Long? Or should I say, Longarm?"

Longarm stiffened. He had his arms stretched out on either side along the tops of the seat-back. His legs were crossed at the ankles and out in front of him. He was in no position to make any moves, sudden or otherwise. He said slowly, "Doc, I reckon you know that guns are dangerous. When you been drinkin' you sure don't want to be fooling around with one."

The doctor smiled. Longarm noticed that he had repaired the bent frames of his glasses. Then the doctor said, "Marshal, that is excellent advice. I want you to reach to your side and grasp the butt of your revolver with two fingers. Just two. I want you to very carefully pull it out of your holster and throw it out of the coach. You are closest to the back, so I suggest you just pitch it out there."

Longarm did not move his hands or his arms. He said, "That would leave you with a gun and I wouldn't have one."

The doctor smiled again and cocked the hammer back on the revolver. "Don't make me get careless, Marshal. This gun doesn't have a particularly fine-tuned hair trigger on it, but this coach is jolting about. A wrong bump and this pistol could go off. I don't think I could miss at this range. Do you? You don't want to bet your life on the nerves of an old drunk. That wouldn't be wise."

Then Longarm saw what had bothered him about the

doctor's eyes. "Hell, you ain't no old drunk! Dammit, I should have seen before."

"Whatever are you talking about, sir?"

"Your eyes, dammit, your eyes! The whites of your damn eyes."

"And what is wrong with the whites of my 'damn' eyes, as you choose to call them?"

Longarm was furious with himself. "They *are* white, that's what the hell is wrong with them. Dammit! If you were an old drunk they'd be bloodshot! I saw it and it bothered me, I just couldn't put my finger on it. Hell, you've been acting. Your eyes are whiter than mine."

The doctor smiled genially. "Well, all that aside, Marshal, this coach continues to jolt its way along and the business end of this revolver is still pointed at your chest. I want you to throw your side arm out of the coach."

Longarm looked down the bench at Rita Ann. She was sitting quietly, serenely, her hands holding her cloth purse in her lap. She seemed detached from what was happening. Longarm figured she was scared. Well, for that matter, so was he. He never had cared to have men he didn't know or understand point loaded pistols at him.

He said, "You're not going to shoot me, Doc. The driver will hear the noise and he'll pull up his team and come to have a look."

The doctor nodded. "That's probably quite true, Marshal. And then you would have a dead driver and a dead guard. Something I am not anxious to have happen. But if I have to shoot you I will have to shoot them also."

"You couldn't drive this team."

The doctor showed a fine set of teeth in a smile. "I'm a very resourceful man, Marshal. You'd be surprised at what I can do if I have to. For that matter I have no desire to shoot a federal marshal. Having the federal service hot after me is nothing I care to add to my troubles. But I am a man with serious business to tend to and you are in the way. I command you one last time to take your revolver out of the holster and throw it overboard.''

Longarm calculated his chances. They didn't look good. The hand that was holding the pistol was steady as a rock, and the doctor looked like a man very willing and capable of pulling a trigger and shooting another man. He glanced again at Rita Ann, surprised she had been so quiet. He thought of the one brief moment of contact they had had that day. It hadn't told him much about her feelings. Not too long before the stage arrived he had gone into the kitchen looking for Mrs. Higgins. She hadn't been there, but Rita Ann had come in immediately and hugged him around the waist. She'd kissed him and put her hand down inside his waistband so that he'd thought they were going to have a repeat of their previous kitchen scene. But she'd just kissed him again and left as quickly as she'd come. She was, he'd decided, a very strange woman.

The doctor said, ''Marshal, nothing you can think to do is going to help. Meanwhile you are getting further and further from the relay station. It will be a long, hot walk as it is. The longer you delay . . .'' The doctor shrugged. ''You could die without water.''

Longarm nodded. It made sense. Without moving he reached carefully to his side and pulled out his revolver as he had been instructed. He held it in the air, dangling from his thumb and forefinger. ''Now what?''

The doctor nodded. ''Throw it out the opening to your side.''

Longarm did as he was told, but it hurt him to see a fine instrument like his revolver thrown into the sand. But now he had to begin working a plan. There was his derringer in his gunbelt buckle, and he had to get the doctor to relax and point his gun somewhere else long enough to get it out and perhaps shoot the man.

But the doctor had further instructions. He said, ''Now the Winchester under your seat. Just lean down, pick it up by the barrel, and pitch it out the back over the tailgate. Do it in one motion.''

"Why?"

"Let's just say it makes me nervous to have surplus weapons about. I'd hurry. I would guess we've come at least two miles from the relay station, if not farther. Now the Winchester."

Longarm shrugged. He sat up straight on the bench and bent low, and with his right hand grasped his carbine by the barrel. For an instant he thought about plunging to the floor and trying for one quick shot, but he quickly dismissed the thought. It hadn't come to that kind of desperate measure yet. The derringer was still his best bet. But he needed to get the doctor talking, get him distracted. He flung the rifle in one smooth motion out the back of the coach, sailing it over the tailgate. He saw it hit in the sandy dirt and bounce and roll and finally stop. It was going to take him forever to get it cleaned up.

He turned back to the doctor and leaned back as if settling in for a long ride. But the doctor said, "You go next, Marshal. I'm fairly certain that I have rendered you harmless. There is no way for you to chase us from the relay station. I've made certain of that. So I think we can do without your company."

But Longarm didn't move. He had dropped his right hand casually into his lap and was working it slowly up toward the top of his buckle. He said, "Doc, one thing I don't understand. The lenses in your glasses look different. How come?"

The doctor smiled slightly. "Oh, that is probably because I'm careless and because I only wear glasses as a sort of disguise. You'd be surprised at the number of people who only remember you as a man wearing glasses. When they see you later without glasses they don't recognize you. These are plain glass. No more magnification than a window glass. But that has nothing to do with the issue at hand. If you don't mind I'd like you to make your way to the end of the coach and slip quietly over the tailgate. At the speed we're making it should be quite safe. As I say, I have no wish to harm

111

you, Marshal, but you are interfering with my business. And I'd remind you, if you call out to the driver, you will surely cause his death. Do I make myself clear?''

Longarm had gotten his thumb inside his belt buckle and was frantically searching for his derringer. He thought it might have escaped from its clip and fallen down, but he couldn't feel anything.

Rita Ann said distinctly, ''Lose something?''

Startled, he turned his head and glanced her way. ''What?''

She reached in her bag and came out holding his derringer. ''Looking for this?''

He stared. ''Son of a bitch,'' he said slowly. He shook his head. ''You sure as hell took me in. I'll be . . . go to hell.''

The doctor laughed quietly. He said, ''Gulled by a woman. Is there anything that is a worse blow to the male pride? Oh, me. I wish you could see the expression on your face, sir. It is a sight. Yessir, it is a sight.'' The doctor laughed again. ''Oh, I know the feeling, sir, and I sympathize with you. But better you than me, I say.''

Longarm looked at Rita Ann, sitting serenely with the derringer dangling from her hand. He said, ''Well, the laugh is on me. You sure took me in all right. I didn't think you were a whore and you turned out to be one after all. I guess I didn't know there were different kinds.'' He nodded toward the doctor. ''This the gambler who left you high and dry in Phoenix, Rita Ann?''

''You can drop the Ann,'' she said. ''I only use that on the rubes.''

''Aaah,'' Longarm said. ''There's more and more to you every time I look. Now I'm a rube. Well, I reckon I'd rather be a rube than what you are.''

A little edge came to her voice. ''Save the sermons for somebody who gives a damn, Mr. Long. Talk about acting. You make me laugh. A rich businessman. You gave yourself away so bad in that fight that it was downright stupid.''

The doctor said, ''Now, now, Rita. No use being unkind. The marshal is like us, only doing his job."

She said, "It burns me up somebody tries to play me for a fool." She gave Longarm a hard look. "Poor little girl in her mousy dress. Get her fixed up and feel like a big man." She made a motion with the derringer. "Go on. Get the hell out of here while you are still in one piece. I ain't as charitable as Doc. I'd like to put a couple of holes in you."

Longarm turned away from her. He said to Peabody, "What's your game, Doc? You ain't planning on robbing this stage, are you? I ain't familiar with this particular line, but I hear they got a pretty good record of foiling robberies."

The doctor gave him a slight smile. "Marshal, I'm sure you will forgive me if I choose not to discuss my business with a federal officer. I'm sure you can understand that." He motioned with the revolver. "You have already caused us a little inconvenience and I think it is time you took your leave. Just slip quietly over the tailgate."

Longarm looked at him. He shifted his weight on the seat, putting it forward on the balls of his feet. "Doc, I don't think you will shoot me. I've stayed alive just on these kind of decisions and I don't think you'll pull that trigger. Like you said, killing a federal officer is a losing game."

From the head of the coach Rita said, coolly, "He may not, but I will."

As he turned his head and looked at her, she pulled back the hammers of the two-shot derringer. He knew they were a hard pull, and he was surprised at the strength in her thumb. She said, "You got about five seconds."

The doctor said, "Marshal Long, you will be endangering the guard and the driver." There was an urgency in his voice. "I cannot always control her. I advise you to go and go quickly."

Longarm looked at the doctor, and then he looked at Rita. He got slowly to his feet, nodding his head. He said quietly, "All right. I'll get off here."

As he made his way to the end of the coach the doctor said, "Don't call out to the driver, Marshal. You know what will happen."

Longarm climbed over the tailgate, standing on the fender. He looked back into the coach. "Maybe that I'll see you two again."

The doctor said, "One other piece of advice, Marshal. I wouldn't risk my health by running back to the relay station in order to send a telegram on ahead. Won't do any good. The lines have been cut."

Longarm nodded. He would like to have said something about Carl Lowe and about what he knew, if for no other reason than to wipe the smug look off their faces. But he knew better than that. The less they knew about what he knew, the better off he was. As it was, things weren't looking all that well. He said, "I'm much obliged for the advice, Doctor. And I wish you good luck. That she-cat you are running with and you are going to need it."

With that he dropped off the coach. It was going slow enough that he was able to stay on his feet by lumbering along in a kind of run for a few seconds. Finally he was able to slow to a walk and then stop. He could just barely see the top of the hats of the driver and the guard as they sat on their perch in front of the box. He realized he didn't know the whole story, but he felt he knew enough that he could still stop it from happening.

But he was once again out in the middle of the Arizona badlands, afoot and with no water.

Chapter 7

For a moment he stared after the stage as if he could stop its progress by sheer will of mind. But the coach kept rolling and there wasn't much time. If he was going to stop the robbery he was going to have to hurry. He turned and started back toward the south, walking fast. But after a few strides he stopped. Walking wasn't going to be fast enough. He calculated he was somewhere between two and three miles from Higgins's relay station. He was going to have to find a way to run. He sat down and pulled off his boots. He didn't know how many rocks or sharp objects there were between where he was and the station, but he'd just have to try and miss them. He figured to run along the road made by the broad wheels of the coach. He took off the belt to his jeans, which he really didn't need anyway, and ran it through the pull-ups on the sides of his boots. He buckled the belt and then put it around his neck, slinging his boots to his back. His gunbelt was heavy, so he unbuckled it and let it fall to the ground. He might get it back later and he might not. He reckoned not was the more likely.

Finally there was nothing to do but strike a trot. He didn't reckon he'd ever run further than a hundred yards since he'd been a boy, but he was about to find out how much stamina he had.

It seemed the further he ran the hotter the sun got. He could almost feel it getting hotter with every stride. On top of the heat outside, he was making heat inside. The only good part to the whole matter was that the air was so dry he didn't sweat. That was good. With no water he could ill afford to lose any more body liquid than he had to.

Within ten minutes he saw his Winchester carbine ahead. He scooped it up without stopping, shaking it as he ran, trying to get the sand out of the gun's action. It probably didn't matter anyway. His chances of catching up with Doc and Rita and the stage were not very good, he calculated. He figured he had a better chance of dying from heatstroke.

The stations were twenty miles apart. If indeed he was a little over two miles from Higgins's station, that meant that the stage had seventeen or eighteen miles to go. He didn't know how long it would take him to reach Higgins's place, or how much progress the stage would make while he was bursting his lungs and frying his brains. There was that long grade and maybe that would slow the stage down, but he had to figure some way of rigging up some sort of conveyance to carry him on his chase. Maybe, he thought, the three gunmen might have returned. If they had, he could take their horses and set out in hot pursuit. If they hadn't, or if there wasn't anyone else there with a horse, he didn't have the slightest idea what he could do. Maybe they could fix the telegraph wires and wire ahead to warn the next station. But he had a feeling that that station was already in Doc's control. He had no way of knowing such a thing for certain, but he had the feeling.

Maybe, he thought, he could find some way to hook two mules together and put some sort of wide sling between them that he could sit on. The thought would have made him laugh if he hadn't needed the breath.

He had to keep switching his rifle from hand to hand.

It was too heavy and too cumbersome to carry with any ease. And his boots kept beating a tattoo on his back. He thought of discarding the rifle in hopes that Higgins might have one at the station, but he couldn't chance it. If he was successful in catching the stage he was going to need the rifle and need it bad.

Fortunately the ground was turning out to be easier going than he'd expected. So long as he kept to the tracks of the stage, all the rocks and other painful things had been mashed down into the soft sand and did him no harm. Even his legs were holding up fairly well.

But it was his breathing that was about to do him in. He couldn't seem to take in enough air to fill his bursting lungs. And with every stride, he could feel the effects of every cigar he'd ever smoked and every drink he'd ever downed. He vowed, if he lived through the run, to live a pure life from that hour forward.

He ran, his eyes fixed on the horizon, praying for the tops of the station buildings to miraculously appear. But he knew he had a long way to go. Dishearteningly, when he thought he must have covered at least a mile, he came across his revolver. He knew the stage hadn't covered a mile since he'd thrown it out. He scooped it up without stopping. He dared not stop. If he stopped he wasn't sure he could start again.

At first he put the revolver in his waistband, but it irritated him and kept trying to slip down. Finally he ended up carrying the rifle in one hand and the revolver in the other. They seemed to balance each other.

He thought of Rita and gritted his teeth. They were sandy. She had pulled a nice little trick on him with that last hug she'd given him. When she'd made as if to put her hand inside his jeans, she'd been reaching for a gun, all right, but it hadn't been the one he'd thought. She'd taken his damn derringer. Well, he would have it back from her and no mistake. He didn't know if he was more angry at her or at himself for the easy way she'd worked him. He reckoned she'd known he was a marshal almost from the first. Either she'd overheard the Higginses talking or she'd found his badge in his shirt pocket.

He kept running, gasping for air, the gasps coming closer and closer together. He couldn't get enough air, and what he could was as dry and hot as a prairie fire. He wanted to stop. He desperately wanted to stop. His legs were starting to get heavy and his arms and shoulders were aching from carrying the weapons. You needed air to breathe and he wasn't sure he was getting enough, or if he was, he was using up more than he was getting. The pain in his throat and chest was intense. He did not think he could go on, but he kept putting one foot in front of the other and taking turns switching the rifle and the revolver from one hand to the other.

He had to find something to hitch a team of mules to. A sled of some kind or a skid. Hell, maybe a bedstead. No, not a bedstead, but what about a mattress ticking? No, that would tear to pieces in the first mile. Maybe the Higginses' little dining room table. Turn it upside down and he'd have the legs to hang on to.

He ran, turning ideas over and over in his mind, trying not to think of his body, which was crying out for him to cease torturing it. He tried thinking of lovers from his past, but that didn't work mainly because he was hurting so bad that he couldn't concentrate, but also because he couldn't get the devious bitch Rita Ann out of his mind. With every stride he said in his head, "The day will come, woman, the day will come. The day with me and you alone and then matters will get settled. The day will come when you will rue you ever heard my name, much less met me, much less used me, much less overpowered me in a way no woman ever has before."

But it was no good. Thinking of her made him angry, and he didn't have any extra energy to waste on anything other than keeping his legs moving. His shirt was too tight across the chest. It felt as if it was constricting him, closing off his lungs. With the hand holding the revolver he made several attempts to rip open the buttons. He finally succeeded on the third try, but the effort was such that it made him stumble and almost fall. That scared

118

him. If he ever fell he wasn't sure he'd be able to get up.

He tried to think about how he would organize matters once he got to the station, what he'd have Higgins looking for to make him some sort of conveyance that could be pulled behind two or four or more mules. Then how to repair the wires. But again, he couldn't concentrate.

And where were the three gunmen? The three he'd sent packing. They had to be part of the plan, but they had not met the stage. Maybe they had gone ahead and taken control of the station the stage was bound for.

It was all too much. He finally quit trying to think at all. He ran. He ran with his head down, looking ahead no more than three or four yards. He ran, staring at the brown, ugly, sandy dirt. He ran with the sound of his own gasping sounding like the roaring surf he'd once heard out in California. He could feel his pulse beating in his temple. It was going like a triphammer. The only time it ever did that, as best he could remember, was in the heat of passion. Well, this sure as hell wasn't the heat of passion. There was heat, heat enough to bake bread and fry steaks, but no passion.

Ripping open his shirt hadn't helped. What was constricting him, he discovered, was not his shirt but the skin of his own chest. And underneath that his ribs were choking him. For the first time he began to think about failure. His body was telling him that it couldn't go on, not for any reason.

Finally he got to the point where he said to himself that he would take just ten more strides and then he would stop. He counted them off in his head, his puffing and gasping coming faster than the count. When he reached ten, he told himself he would just go ten more and then definitely stop. But when that ten was up he made a deal with himself that he would run ten more strides and then he would look up. If he could not see some little part of the relay station he would stop. Maybe he would keep on walking, but he would stop running.

He counted off the ten strides and then very slowly

raised his eyes. Nothing but desolate badlands met his eyes. There was nothing in sight that looked like the hand of man had ever touched it with the exception of the coach tracks. He could stop now, he thought, with honor. He *should* stop. He was going to die if he didn't stop. He wanted, he needed, it was necessary to stop.

He kept running. Now, burning his mind like an image that would never fade was every laugh that damn woman had had on him. Well, he would have the last laugh or he would die in worn-out socks.

He raised his eyes. There, directly ahead, he could see the buildings of the relay station. Not just the tops of the buildings, but all of them. All of them and the front yard. Somehow he had struggled up some sort of rise in the prairie and topped it and then there, right in front of him, was the relay station. It was downhill all the way to the front door.

But he was starting to stagger. His legs felt like they were made of lead and not really connected to him. Of their own choice they seemed to want to go wandering off in different and odd directions that had nothing to do with his intentions for them. He didn't know how far away the buildings were. Between the film of exhaustion over his eyes and the shimmering heat waves, he couldn't tell if they were a half mile away or a week. All he could do was keep on the way he'd come, putting one foot in front of the other.

He put his head down and went back to staring at the ground, guiding his steps by the tracks of the stage. His legs were getting limp and his shoulders were aching so bad from carrying the guns that he didn't think he could stand it much longer. For some reason he had started breathing easier. It was as if something had finally burst under the pressure and he had a greater capacity to suck in the dry, hot air.

He raised his eyes, concentrating on the main building of the station. It seemed he could see someone standing under the porch, very near the front door. He looked down at the sand again and did not raise his eyes again until he'd counted off thirty strides. Yes, there was definitely someone there. If his vision had been normal he felt almost certain he would have been able to see the figure clearly. Then a distant noise seemed to come to his ears, like someone shouting. Through his squinted eyes he saw the figure come out of the shade of the porch and start toward him. It was Higgins. He was waving his arms and yelling, but Longarm couldn't make out the words for the roaring in his ears and the sound of his gasping breaths. Then he saw that Higgins had broken into a kind of trot, running to meet him. He wanted to make some sort of signal, but he couldn't raise either hand, not and hold on to his weapons.

Now he could see clearly that he was not that far from the station. Desert air was known for playing tricks on your vision, but he could tell it was no more than two hundred yards away. And Higgins was coming on, the distance between them narrowing. Then he finally heard Higgins's voice. He was yelling as he bounced up and down in his peculiar run, "Marshal Long! Longarm! Mister Long! Marshal! What's wrong? What happened?"

Longarm slogged along grimly, thinking that Higgins must have never been out of breath if he thought you could run and yell at the same time. At least after you'd run better than two miles under the desert sun. He was dying to know what time it was, but he couldn't look at his watch. He'd had one look at it just before the doctor had pulled out his pistol. It was about a mile after they'd left the station. His watch had said forty minutes after three. But then he didn't know how much time had elapsed before he'd finally gotten out of the coach. It couldn't have been much, not a great deal more than five minutes. Perhaps ten at the most. He had to remember to look at the time when he got to the station. It was very important that he know what kind of a lead the stage had.

Then Higgins reached him. For a moment the old man danced around in front of Longarm like the runner was going to stop. Finally, when Longarm had to go to the trouble to circle him, he fell in stride to Longarm's left asking what had happened, what was going on, what and where was the trouble, and why was Longarm running.

Longarm knew he didn't have much breath to spare, but he thought if he could get the old man to run ahead and have something prepared for him, it would save trouble. He got the words out one at a time, between gasping breaths, each one coming out as slowly and painfully from his parched throat as if they were being pulled from him with red-hot tongs. He said, "Hurry . . . to . . . station . . . fix . . . me . . . big . . . glass . . . water. Put . . . some . . . whiskey . . . in . . . it. Hurry."

But Higgins didn't go. He said, "But what's it all about, Marshal? What's happened?"

The world was starting to turn dim, even in the blinding sunlight. "Can't . . . talk. No . . . breath. Hurry . . . dying . . . of . . . thirst."

Finally the old man seemed to get the message. He said, "You want me to run on ahead and get you a big glass of water and put a little whiskey in it?"

All Longarm could do was nod mutely. But he did hold out his rifle to the old man. Higgins stared at it for a second and then took it. He said, "Yessir, I'm going to run fast as I can an' fix yore water. Longarm, it ain't healthy running in this sun."

Longarm turned blazing eyes on him. He couldn't speak, but his eyes said a lot. Higgins nodded his head. "Yessir! I'm a-goin'! An' right now!"

He put his head down as Higgins, surprisingly agile, raced on ahead. When he looked up after twenty strides the man was out of sight. But by now he could distinctly see the shade cast by the porch roof. It was the most inviting sight he thought he'd ever seen. He kept running. It was odd, but even though he'd given his carbine to Higgins, he could still feel the weight of the weapon in his hand and arm and shoulder. He kept running, starting now to stagger more than just a little. Sometimes he had trouble finding and following the coach track. The whole world seemed to be going gray.

And then he suddenly felt cool. He blinked and looked up. He had run under the porch and was about to run into the wall of the station. He stopped. At least he stopped moving his legs, though they felt as if they were still in motion. The door to the station was just a few feet to his left. With the last of his strength he took the few strides to it and then turned into the incredibly dim and cool interior of the station. Higgins was coming toward him holding out a quart jar full of what looked to be water colored with a little whiskey. Longarm made it as far as the bench by the front door and then he collapsed. Higgins said in alarm, "My laws, Marshal, I believe you have overdone yoreself."

When he could he gasped out the main elements of what had happened. Mrs. Higgins stood alongside her husband looking very upset and concerned. Her only reaction was to say, "Oh, not Rita Ann! Not that sweet girl! Oh, no, I can't believe it!"

He drank down the first jar of water and whiskey very carefully, taking it in small sips, forcing himself to take it slow when his whole body was screaming out for him to dump the precious stuff down his throat. But he persevered. It took him perhaps five minutes. Then Higgins brought him another jar with a little more whiskey. He sipped at it slowly while he tried to tell them as much as he could. The water and whiskey were helping, but he could tell just how done in his body was. He hurt all over, and he knew it would only get worse. But all that didn't matter. Right then time was the most important factor. When he had told Higgins about the plan to rob the stage, the stationkeeper wanted to run to telegraph the news to his company. When Longarm said the wires had been cut, Higgins insisted on going in and trying his key. It didn't matter, since Longarm was going to need at least half an hour to recover. He gave his rifle to Mrs. Higgins and told her she needed to eject the cartridges and clean the sand off whatever she could. Then Higgins came back looking glum. He said, "Yep. You be right. Wires is cut both north and south. My key is as dead as a doornail. What the hell we gonna do, Marshal."

Longarm's breathing was almost back to normal. Mrs. Higgins brought him some cooking grease and he greased his feet and put his boots back on. But they were a snug fit, and he took them off again. His feet had swelled and his socks, even worn out as they were, were too thick. Mrs. Higgins brought him a pair of her husband's thin white cotton socks. He put them on and then his boots fit better.

He said to both of them, "Look, I don't have much time. Mrs. Higgins, you see to my guns and fix me something easy to eat. Stir up some eggs in some milk with some sugar. That ought to work. Half a dozen eggs in a quart of milk. Mister Higgins, you've got to go out and get your Mexicans to harness the most reliable span of mules you've got. The easiest to handle."

Higgins scratched his head. "Wa'l, that be fine. I got just the mules, but we ain't got no harness fer just the one span."

Longarm stifled the urge to scream. He said calmly, "Mister Higgins, Herman, I ain't got but a little time. You'll have to cut some harness down to fit one span."

"Cut company harness?"

Then Longarm couldn't hold it in any longer. "Dammit, Herman, a bunch of robbers is fixing to steal how many thousands of dollars in gold from your company and you are talking to me about cutting up some damned harness!" He suddenly stopped and took a breath. Mrs. Higgins was coming in with his rifle. He said, "Look here, I'm sorry I yelled, but I ain't got a lot of time or strength. I'm nearly done in. So you got to do what I tell you without explaining or arguing."

Higgins said, "My stars, Marshal, I don't know what went through my mind. Sylvie, I'm losing my reason. Course we can cut a harness down to fit a span of mules, but what you gonna hitch them up to?"

Longarm shook his head. "I don't know. Some kind

124

of sled. I thought about your little table, but I'm scared it would just dig in the dirt and flip over. I'll think of something. Right now run out and get those Mexicans busy hooking me up a team." As Higgins started out of the room, Longarm took the Winchester from Mrs. Higgins and ejected the cartridges by working the lever action. It hurt him to hear the gritty sound of the action as he worked the receiver chamber back and forth. But it made him think of something. He said to Higgins, "Herman, you ain't got any forty-four-caliber shells by any chance, do you?"

Higgins stopped and nodded. "Happens I do. Got a fairly fresh box of 'em. Got an old rifle myself, though the sights need straightening."

"Don't let me forget them," Longarm said. Both his revolver and rifle fired .44 cartridges, but all his extra ammunition was in his saddlebags, which were on top of the stage. He said, "Hurry those Mexicans up. Every minute that stage is getting closer and closer to the next station."

Mrs. Higgins had picked up the cartridges. She said, "I'll clean these right up and do what I can for your guns. But hadn't I better bring you your eggs and milk first?"

Longarm slumped back on the bench. "Yeah, I reckon. Faster I get it down the faster it will help me get some strength back. But what I'd like to do is get out back and pump a bucket of water and douse myself down. Don't know if I got the strength, though."

Mrs. Higgins said, "Why, I can do better than that. Why don't you go in there and get in our Sears and Roebuck galvanized bathtub and turn on the tap from that pipe that runs up to the cistern on the roof. You can be resting and soaking the heat out of your poor body while you are at it. And you don't even have to take your clothes off. Maybe yore boots. Wouldn't want to get them wet. And I can bring you your milk and eggs right there and you can rest and soak and eat all the same time."

"Sylvia," he said, "that's a damn good idea." He heaved himself to his feet, doing it quickly to catch his body off guard. For a second he stood swaying, the room moving around him. He still had the sensation he was running. He stood a moment until he was certain he wasn't going to fall, and then followed Mrs. Higgins through their private quarters and back to the curtained-off bathroom and its bathtub.

There was a little rubber plug in the bottom of the tub. Mrs. Higgins put it in place, saying that they just let the tub drain out on the floor and then the slope of the floor took it outside. She turned the tap and slightly brownish water began running into the tub. He sat on the edge and took his boots off, relishing the idea of cooling off his still-overheated body. The tub wasn't all that deep, maybe two feet or a little more at its lowest point. But it curved up toward the other end to make a backrest where you could lean back and put your legs out straight and kind of soak the lower part of your body. But since the tub wasn't much more than four feet long, he reckoned if you wanted to soak the upper half of yourself you'd have to slide down and kind of put your legs in the air. It wasn't all that wide either, at least not down toward the bottom, and he wasn't sure if his shoulders would fit in the bottom.

But it was as good a way as any to refresh himself. He swung around and eased his body into the half-full tub, carefully keeping his stocking feet out of the water. By putting his feet on the top of the lower end he could slide down into the tub to where the water was halfway between his waist and his chest. It felt wonderfully cool. Mrs. Higgins brought him his glass of cool milk with the eggs and sugar mixed in, and he sat there savoring it, sipping it at first and then taking long drinks. All it needed, he decided, was a little whiskey to make it maybe the best drink he'd ever had in his entire life. Even with it only half drunk he could feel strength returning. All of a sudden he remembered the time. He put his hand in his right-hand shirt pocket and jerked

126

out his watch. The time read forty minutes after four. He mulled it over in his mind. He'd actually made pretty good time on his run. Only an hour or less had passed since the good doctor had drawn his gun. He did some calculations in his head, though his mind was still a little groggy. If the mule team was making five or six miles an hour, that meant they would have gone on another five miles or so from where he had gotten off the stage. Figure he had been three miles from the station, that made eight miles. The team still had twelve miles to go to reach the next relay station, and that up a bad grade where they would more than likely slow down to something under four miles an hour. He had a chance. It wasn't a good one, but if he could find something to ride that the mules could pull at a fast clip, he might just catch the stage.

He put his head back and stared up at the ceiling, reliving the run he had just made. He shuddered. He didn't know how he'd done it and he'd never do it again, even if it meant a raise in pay and the right to every woman in Denver.

Lying back, he let his skin absorb the water. He doubted if his pores were actually drinking it in, but he *knew* he didn't feel so dried out, and it hadn't been much more than a quarter of an hour ago when he figured he could have passed for a big chunk of beef jerky.

He finished his milk and eggs and set the jar on the floor next to the tub. He worked his body down as far as he could. He'd thought his shoulders wouldn't fit the width of the tub, but it was wider than he'd thought. He lay there, staring up at the ceiling, trying to think of how he was going to catch up to the stage. If he could just think of something he could hitch the mules to. It made him want to shake his head in disbelief that a place as out of the way as a relay station wouldn't at least have a buckboard or a buggy, never mind a saddle horse. What in hell were the residents supposed to do if they had to get around or go for help or needed to borrow some sugar or salt from the nearest neighbors? Well, he could understand it from the stage company's viewpoint. It kept your stationkeepers in place, but he didn't think it was very humane.

A thought suddenly came to him. He let it lay for a moment, just floating around in his head, and then brought it forward and gave it serious consideration. Abruptly, he sat up and turned around and looked at the back of the bathtub, the way it curved up, like the prow of a ship. The foot of the tub was the same. It curved upward. He suddenly scrambled out of the tub, excited, dripping water all over the place. He could clearly see that the tub was curved upwards in all parts of it, including the sides. The only flat part was the very bottom, and it was only about two feet wide. There wasn't a single angle to snag or dig into the dirt. He ran out of the bathroom, yelling. He shouted, "Mrs. Higgins! Mrs. Higgins!"

The matronly lady came huffing in from the front room looking alarmed. She said, "Marsha—I mean, Cust—I mean, Mr. Long, is something wrong?"

"No, everything is fine. Listen, I need to stay out of the sun as much as I can. Will you run outside and tell Herman to come and to bring his Mexicans with him."

She stared at him. "Why, yes, of course. Is something wrong?"

He pointed back at the bathtub. "How do you get the water out of this thing?"

She said, "Why you just pull that little black rubber plug there. It will run out. The floor slopes to the back."

"Well, would you please get Mister Higgins. I've got to get moving, Sylvia."

She frowned slightly. "Now you're sure you are all right? You had a good bit of that sun, you know."

"I know I did, Sylvia, but I'm all right. I'm just in a hurry. And when you get around to it, I wish you'd fill me a big canteen of water and maybe put any bread or biscuits you got left over in a bag. Piece of ham or something to go with it."

She said, "I'll get Mr. Higgins right away."

Chapter 8

Higgins stood in the bathroom and stared at Longarm. He said, "You want to do *what* with my wife's bathtub?"

"Use it as a sled, a kind of sleigh. It's the only thing around here I can think of that will work. See how rounded it is on the bottom? See how the sides slope outward? Be like riding in a soup dish. This thing will go skimming over that flat desert faster than if it had wheels."

Higgins blinked. "But that's Sylvie's *bathtub*! You want to have some mules drag that thing across the desert? Mister Long, she ain't had it six months yet. Was the desire of her heart. She'd been takin' baths in a number-two washtub fer years. An' now you want to, to, to . . ." He stopped, unable to go on, and rolled his eyes in his head.

Longarm said briskly, "Herman, time is wasting. I got to get hitched up and get going. I'll see she gets this one back or another one."

Higgins said, "It would break her heart, Marshal. She—"

A voice behind him said, "Herman, if the marshal needs that bathtub, you let him take it on. My goodness, he's after shore-'nough criminals. He could get hisself kilt and I don't know what else. Marshal, you are more than welcome to that tub. I can get by without it.''

Longarm said, "Thank you, Sylvia." Then he turned to Higgins. "Herman, get your Mexicans in here to get this thing outside. Have them put it in front of the station. That's where I figure to leave from."

Higgins shrugged. "Shoot, Marshal, me an' you can tote it. It don't weigh all that much. Sixty, eighty pounds."

Longarm shook his head. "Herman, I got just so much energy left, and I can't spare an ounce for anything except trying to catch up with that stage."

"Go on, Mr. Higgins, like he says," said Mrs. Higgins. "Marshall, I guess it be all right to call you that now, seein' as how we are a-chasin' an evil bunch together. I got yore firearms cleaned up as best I can, though I never took on to put the bullets back in 'em.''

Longarm thanked her. "I'll be doing that while Mr. Higgins is getting the bathtub out front. What about the harness, Herman? You get it cut down?"

Higgins was nearly out of the bathroom. He said, "Yeah, I reckon." Then he glanced at the bathtub. "Though it beats the hell outten me how we gonna hook up that thing." He heaved a sigh. "But I reckon I'll think of somethin'. Sylvie always said I was a figgerin' man."

"Oh, he is, Marshal. My Mr. Higgins will sit an' study on somethin' you think they ain't no way to fix or make right or get built or any of that. Pretty soon he'll get up an' he'll have her figgered out and it'll work too."

Longarm said, "Herman, don't forget that box of forty-four cartridges. When I come out the front door I don't want to come back in. I'm heading north as soon as I step out of here."

Mrs. Higgins said, "I'll sack you up somethin' to eat and fill you a canteen."

Longarm sat in the bathroom on the side of the tub

130

and pulled on his boots. His clothes were soaked from his ankles to his shoulders, but he knew they'd dry in five minutes once he got out the door.

He was out in the common room drinking water with a little whiskey in it when the Mexicans, followed by Mister Higgins, walked past him carrying the bathtub. He picked up his weapons, the sack of food Mrs. Higgins had fixed, the box of cartridges, and the big two-quart canteen, and followed them outside, still sipping at the glass of whiskey water.

The Mexicans set the bathtub down and then stepped back and looked at Higgins. Higgins looked at Longarm. He said, "She pointin' in the right direction? I mean, you want to hitch to the low end or the high one?"

.Longarm carefully placed his load in the bottom of the tub and stepped back and sipped at his drink. He still felt thirsty, though he thought it was more in his mind than his body. He said, "Looks about right to me. I figure to hitch to the low end, however we do it. And I want to snub it up pretty close so the front end will actually rise up a little. Won't be as much drag that way. So, yeah, I'd say it's sitting about right. Might swing that front end a little more toward the stage tracks. I got an idea that when we leave here those mules ain't going to be all that easy to guide."

Higgins rolled his eyes and said, "You ain't jus' whistlin' Dixie, Marshal. I don't quite know how those mules are gonna take to this contraption." But then he spoke to the Mexicans, and they swiveled the bathtub around so it was lined up with the stage tracks.

"Where are the mules?" Longarm asked.

Higgins jerked his head. "The boys got them tied to the corral fence."

"They rested?"

Higgins leveled his eyes on Longarm. "Them mules is got as much go in 'em as a steam locomotive leavin' a lumberyard. I ain't envyin' you this little ride you are fixing to take."

"Well, have you figured out a way to hitch them up?"

Higgins frowned and crossed his arms and stared at the tub. He said, "First thang that come to my mind was we might's well forget 'bout the trace straps. Ain't no place to hook 'em. Best I can figure is knock a little hole in the front of that tub with a hammer and chisel. Then take and run the trace chain through it and stick a big nail or bolt through a link of the chain so it can't go back out the hole."

Longarm said, "Hell, Herman, you are a figgerin' man. That will work. Hell, yes, that will work. Let's get it done. By the way, I want you to put a spade bit in at least one of them mules' mouth."

Mister Higgins nodded and spat. "Done thought of it. Be your near mule. The mule on yore left-hand side." He spat again and looked at the tub and shook his head. "Beats the hell out of me what a man gets up to in the law bid'ness." He turned and gave the Mexicans a volley of instructions in Spanish. They immediately took off for the back.

Longarm said, "I know how much your wife is giving up here. But I'll see she gets a new bathtub."

Higgins snorted. "I didn't know what I was sayin' thar in the bathroom. Hell, yes, we want to catch them crooks. I taken a look at my telegraph wahr. Hell, they done tore it all to pieces. Gonna take some fixin' to get it back up an' workin'. I tell you, Marshal, it makes me feel plumb lonesome with that telegraph wahr cut. Never knowed how much I depended on it. Was like a neighbor to me."

Longarm said, "I forgot a bottle of whiskey. I guess I better take some."

"Snakes out thar," Higgins said.

When Longarm came back, the Mexicans had brought the team around. The mules looked contrary and suspicious and spooky. A Mexican had one each by the head harness, but they were still having trouble controlling them. They got the mules up in front of the bathtub, and then tried to back them into place, but the mules weren't having any of it. They snorted and reared and kicked out with their hind legs.

Higgins said matter-of-factly, "Them mules ain't never seen no bathtub before, let alone set in to pull one. Mules as a general rule don't like new thangs, and that bathtub is mighty new to them."

Longarm could see bandannas hanging out of the Mexicans' pockets. He said to Higgins, "Tell them to blindfold them."

Higgins spoke to them in Spanish and they nodded in agreement and said, "Sí, sí. Es bueno."

Working with one mule at a time, they were able to cover their eyes with their big handkerchiefs. As soon as the mules couldn't see, they got quiet. Higgins laughed. "You must be an old mule man yoreself."

Longarm shook his head. "Never handled one in my life. This will be the first, heaven help me. But it works with horses." He nodded at the hammer and chisel one of the Mexicans had given Higgins. "Hadn't you better knock a hole in the front before we get the mules too close?"

"That's good thinkin', Marshal. Right good thinkin'." He stepped to the front of the tub and measured with his eye. "Say you want the front to ride off the ground a mite?"

"I think that would be good," Longarm said. "But I think we are guessing here. You ain't never hooked mules up to a bathtub and I never drove mules before, bathtub or not."

Higgins said, "I figure about here." He put his finger on a spot about five to six inches down from the top of the lower end.

"Looks fine to me," Longarm said. "Like I say, I think we are guessing."

Higgins set his chisel point and then struck the other end with the hammer. The galvanized tin dented, but it didn't break. "Tougher than it looks."

He set the point of the chisel in the dent and then hit it another blow. A small hole appeared in the surface of the bathtub. Higgins leaned around to look inside. " 'Bout one more ought to do her."

With the next blow, a hole about the size of a quarter appeared on the inside wall of the bathtub. Higgins looked at it. "That ought to 'bout do it. Trace chain will go through there right snug like."

Longarm watched as he took the end of the trace chain, a linked chain with links about an inch and a half long and three quarters of an inch wide, and ran it through the hole. When he had about a foot inside the tub he looked at Longarm. "Now you got to say how close you want the front of this tub to the end of them mules."

Longarm frowned. "Hell, Herman, I ain't got the slightest idea. Have your men start backing the mules up and you take up the slack while I see."

Higgins spoke to the Mexicans, and they urged the mules backwards. The animals stepped backward trembling and reluctant. As they came closer, Higgins pulled on the trace chain that ran to the singletree, a wooden device that kept the mules spaced apart, taking up the slack and letting it lay in the bottom of the tub. Ordinarily, if they had been hitching a wagon or a buckboard, it would have been done with leather straps. The trace chain was only a safety measure in case one of the traces, or leather straps, should break. But since there was no other way to attach the bathtub, they were using the chain only, which gave Longarm very limited control over the team.

When the mules were about three feet from the front of the tub, Higgins told the Mexicans to stop. He said, "I wouldn't jam 'em up any tighter than that."

"Have they got room to run snubbed up that close?" Longarm asked.

Higgins spat. He'd said he always got a mouthful of saliva when he was nervous and the entire affair was making him nervous. "Most folks get a dry mouth when they get jittery. I get spit."

Now he said, "They got just about the right amount

of room to run. You get any further back and they likely to sling you around like a turnip on the end of a string."

Longarm shrugged. "Hell, I'd rather go by train, but it don't look like I got much choice. Hook 'em up."

Higgins took a big nail out of his pocket and ran it through the link just inside the hole in the tub. Then he took a pair of pliers out of his back pocket and bent the nail so it couldn't slip out of the link. He gave a yank on the chain from the outside of the tub and pronounced it solid. "That chain won't break and that tub won't break. These here mules is hitched to this tub until somebody comes along and unhitches 'em." He peered at Longarm. "Course I ain't promising that you is gonna stay part of the outfit. Right now these mules don't know what they hitched to. I ain't right shore how they gonna react once they find out. You better go ahead and get in there and I'll hand you the reins."

One of the Mexicans said something to Higgins, and he nodded. "*Bueno, muy bueno. Vamoose!*"

The Mexican tore off for the barn, and Longarm asked what all that was about. Higgins said, "We got an old coach whip in the feed house. Miguel thought you might make good use of it."

"What's a coach whip?" Longarm thought he knew, but he wanted to be sure.

"Aw, it's a little thin pole 'bout six feet long with about a three-foot leather snapper on the end. See, I don't think you goin' to be able to steer these here mules as much as you'd like to think. So I reckon you are gonna have to lean forward and slap one of 'em on the jaw opposite the way you want to go. You gonna have four reins, but you likely to pull yore arms outten the sockets tryin' to get these here cold-jawed sonsabitches to gee and haw."

Longarm stepped gingerly into the bathtub and worked his way into a sitting position. He was up close to the front of the tub with his legs sort of crossed under him. Higgins walked down by the side of the mules, straightening the harness and letting out the reins. He

135

handed them to Longarm. There were four, two for each mule. Longarm said, "I ain't all that sure I know how to handle this bunch of leather."

Higgins shook his head sorrowfully. "Unfortunately, Marshal, ain't nobody can teach you. Not in that getup you be in. I reckon you are gonna learn on the job. Here comes yore coach whip."

He took the leather-wrapped thin wand from the Mexican and handed it to Longarm. He said, "Try that on for size. See if you can reach them mules' heads."

Longarm extended the coach whip. It went very easily up to where he could pop either mule on either side of his head. He said, "Yeah. I can reach them. I just hope I know what to do at the time I'm supposed to do it."

"You got everything?"

Longarm looked around. His guns and ammunition and food and water were aboard, as well as the little sack of food and the bottle of whiskey. He said, "Let me get in a quick drink before you turn them loose."

"Better make it a good one. Might be the last you have for a time."

Longarm took a hard pull of the bottle and then corked it. He laid it down beside him in the bathtub and then nodded his head. He had one set of reins in one hand and another in the other. He had the whip in his right hand. He pulled his hat on tighter and nodded. He said, "Take off the blindfolds."

The Mexicans untied the hankerchiefs and whipped them away, stepping back quickly. For a moment the mules stood stock still. They both switched their ears back and forth and trembled, but other than that, didn't move. Higgins said, "Shake the reins at 'em. But gently."

Longarm was about to do that, or thinking about doing it, when the off leader turned his head to the inside and walleyed the strange-looking contraption right at his heels. In that instant Higgins yelled, "Don't let 'em look back! It'll spook 'em. Use the whip!"

But it was too late. With a squeal of irritation from the off leader the team suddenly broke into a stampede. One second they were standing there, and the next they seemed to be at a dead run. If he hadn't been holding the reins with both hands Longarm would have tumbled over on his back. As it was, it was all he could do to keep his balance and keep his hat on his head. He had reins in both hands and was set back against them as hard as he could pull, but it made the mules not the slightest bit of difference. Outside the bathtub the desert was whizzing by, and the tub itself was making a sound like bacon frying as it flew over the crusty sand and bits of grass and the occasional rock and cactus.

From behind Longarm heard Higgins yelling, "Rein 'em in! Rein 'em in!"

He wished Higgins was sitting where *he* was sitting, in the bottom of a bathtub with two runaway mules in front of him. He wouldn't have been so quick to yell, "Rein 'em in! Rein 'em in!"

There was no reining the mules in. Fortunately, they were sticking to the stage tracks, so they were going where Longarm wanted to go, except they were going a little faster than he cared for. He was afraid they would play out before he caught the stage at the pace they were setting. But for the time being, he thought the best thing to do was just let them get their run out. Maybe when they tired a little they'd become slightly more manageable.

As they raced along he took stock of the situation. Looking back, he could see the station receding rapidly in the distance. Already the horizon was cutting off Higgins and his two Mexicans at the waist, and in another moment they'd be swallowed up. All the stuff he had brought along was rattling around, but it seemed to be doing all right. It was a strange sensation to him to be sitting so close to the ground at such a speed.

The tub seemed to be pulling all right. As it raced across uneven ground it would sway and bump, but it was hitched too close to the mules to have much play, even on the single trace. Occasionally the tub would go over a rise or a clump of grass and actually get off the ground, landing with a bump, but mostly it seemed to stick pretty close to the ground, remaining stable and acting as he'd envisioned.

But it was bothering the mules. From time to time one or the other would take a wild-eyed look back at this monstrous thing that was dogging their heels and redouble its efforts. Finally, Longarm got comfortable enough to reach forward with the coachman's whip and slap the mules on the cheek to keep them from looking back.

He knew he had to find some way to slow the animals down. Neither horse nor mule nor dog could run as fast as they were running for very long, and he figured he had at least fifteen miles to go to catch up with the coach. He started by bracing his boots against the front of the tub and pulling as hard as he could against the headlong flight of the mules. It made them bow their necks a little, but it didn't slow them down. Their ears were still flicking back and forth in all directions.

Then they suddenly spooked to the right and started off to the east. The move caught Longarm so off guard that he almost fell out of the tub. When he regained his balance he saw that they were heading rapidly away from his intended track. He pulled hard on the rein of the near leader, trying to pull him back to the left, to the west, back toward the stage road. The result only got him a very grudging turn in that direction that might, if given enough time, bring them back on track just before they reached Phoenix. But he couldn't wait that long. He reached forward and slapped the off leader on the right cheek. That brought quick results. The mule turned back to his left, taking his mate with him. Only they were turning too far. As they were crossing the northern line that Longarm wanted, he reached out again and tapped the near leader on the left cheek. The mules broke to the right. He kept that up until he finally had them back on the stage road and heading where he wanted them to go.

And it seemed as if they had slowed down. He gave a healthy pull on both reins, and the mules responded by settling back into a reasonable gallop. It was still too fast, but he thought they would slow down naturally as they tired.

He saw something ahead in the road, brown against the whitish sand. He doubted that it could be, but it looked like his gunbelt, the gunbelt he'd dropped when he'd started his run. If it was, it would give him a pretty good idea of how far he'd come and how far he had to go.

The brown spot turned into a gunbelt and came up very fast. The mules were on a perfect line, so Longarm did nothing to turn them. He leaned over the side of the tub as they whizzed by and reached down and scooped up his gunbelt. It was impossible to believe, and he didn't think he would ever tell the story about the time he'd retrieved his gunbelt while sitting in a bathtub being pulled by a pair of mules across the Arizona desert. There were some tales you told and some you didn't. Not if you wanted to maintain any sort of reputation as a halfway truthful person.

He got his watch out and looked at it. It was six-fifteen. He figured he'd covered five or six miles, maybe more. The mules had settled down to a steady lope and he figured they were making about seven miles an hour. That meant that if he didn't come up to the coach in the next two hours, he wouldn't catch them before they got to the station and got forted up. That would make his job a lot more difficult. Also, it would be starting to get dark in less than two hours, and the only way he had of finding his way was by the tracks of the stage, and he wouldn't be able to see them in the lowering light. He settled down for the ride, grimly hoping the mules would hold out, that something would delay the coach, that he would catch

...em in time. He wanted Carl Lowe, but even more, he wanted Doctor Peabody, if that was his name, and especially Miss Rita Ann. He did not normally take a personal approach to his business as a lawman, but this time he was going to make an exception.

He sped on. The mules seemed to have adjusted to their roles as pullers of a bathtub, and were even responding moderately well to the reins. Without too much tugging and pulling he could keep them on the path whenever the coach tracks curved or went around a patch of rough ground. He dared not completely let go of the reins, but he was able to hold them in one hand while he used the other to have a drink of whiskey and a pull of water and eat a couple of biscuits stuffed with ham. His body seemed to have revived from the punishment he'd given it a few hours before, and he almost believed he could make a fight of it if it came to that.

A half hour later he saw a couple of dark spots lying across the white stretch of the sandy track. At first he was unable to make out what they might be, but as he got closer, he could see that they had to be bodies. But of what he wasn't sure until he was about a quarter of a mile off. Then he could see that it was two men. As he got closer he saw that they were lying on their backs. He was going to pass just at their feet, and he took the reins in both hands and set his boots against the front of the bathtub and pulled with all his might. The mules slowed to a stiff-legged trot, but that was as slow as he could get them. As he passed the two men, Longarm recognized Ben, the driver, and the shotgun guard. In the brief glimpse he had of them he could see, judging from the blood, that both had been shot several times. He closed his eyes and clenched his jaws and relaxed his iron grip on the reins, letting the mules build back up to their high-ended lope.

He didn't know why he was surprised, much less outraged, that they'd killed the driver and the guard. The good doctor and Rita Ann weren't going to let anything get between them and the gold. Hell, they would have killed Longarm just as quick as they'd have swatted a fly if they hadn't figured the desert would do for him and that he was in no position to impede them. And the doctor had been right about the business of killing federal marshals. It was bad medicine to kill a federal officer. You did it only if you wanted every other federal officer in the country to be looking for you, because that was what would happen.

He only wondered how they had done it. It would have been difficult for either of them to climb around and get at the driver or the guard. Likely they had used some sort of subterfuge, the doctor saying the woman was sick or something like that. Anything to get the driver and guard to stop and get down and be exposed to the doctor's revolver.

But why kill them so far from the station? Longarm already knew that driving mules was no picnic, and he was just having to manage two. The doctor would be handing ten. Maybe it was a lot easier from the seat of the coach. Maybe the mules had worn down and were manageable. Who knows what the reason was. Maybe they just liked to kill for the hell of it.

And then he got his answer about half an hour later. They came flying over a slight rise and started down into a little low place in the prairie. Well off in the distance he saw the stage. It was pulling up the gradually rising grade the driver had talked about. But that wasn't what explained the situation to him. There were three riders accompanying the coach. One was out ahead, one rode just to the right, and a third was bringing up the rear. Longarm estimated they were a good three or four miles away, but he knew he was going faster. He calculated he should come up to them in something less than a half an hour. But he figured that long before that the outriders were going to take a big interest in him, and for that he was going to need the use of both hands.

He hunted around in the bottom of the tub until he

found his recently retrieved gunbelt. He looped it loosely around his chest, buckling it just under his armpits. Then he took the extra slack in the reins, ran them under and around his gunbelt, and tied them off. That way he could control the speed of the team by leaning forward or pulling back.

He was coming up on the party faster than he'd thought. He could see the last outrider stop his horse and turn in Longarm's direction. Longarm took up his carbine, levered the chamber half open to make sure a shell was home, and then closed it and cocked the hammer with his thumb. He said to the mules, "I don't know if you boys have ever been in a gunfight before, but you are fixing to be smack in the middle of one. But don't worry about it. I'm an old hand at the business. Ya'll just keep pulling the bathtub and I'll see to the shooting."

Now the distance was narrowing rapidly. The trailing rider had made his mind up and was starting toward Longarm at a trot. As he came on, Longarm saw him pull his rifle out of the boot and glance down to check the action. Up further the man riding by the stage also had stopped and was turning back. Longarm estimated he was no more than a half mile from the closest rider and closing fast. He watched as the man put his horse into a lope, quartering just off to Longarm's right. It was still too far for a certain shot, but the time was getting very close.

Then, as the first man came within about four hundred yards, Longarm saw him stand up in the stirrups, lift his rifle to his shoulder, and aim. Then there came a puff of smoke, and Longarm saw a red furrow appear across the hip of the off-leader mule. It wasn't a serious wound, and the mule did no more than jump slightly, but Longarm suddenly realized what kind of shape he'd be in if the man managed to kill one of his animals. He'd be out of business was what he'd be. His quarry would get away and he'd be stuck out in the middle of the desert for a third time.

"The hell with that!" he said softly. He raised his rifle to his shoulder and sighted on the chest of the man riding toward him.

Chapter 9

The instant he fired, he knew that he had missed. He also knew why. He had a more stable firing platform than did the man on the horse, but he hadn't allowed for shooting at a moving target from a moving object. It wasn't something he got a great deal of practice at.

He quickly levered in another shell and aimed lower on the man's chest. He was quartering in from Longarm's right, and Longarm allowed for a touch of lead as the distance closed. Before he could fire he saw the white puff of smoke from the man's rifle and heard the bullet sing over his head. Then the hard *crump* of the shot reached his ears. The man was close enough now that Longarm could see it was the big man from the relay station, the one he had hit first. He was glad to find out that he had not jumped on three innocent strangers. He was also glad to have been proved right that they were to be a part of the robbery. He squeezed the trigger, felt the kick of the rifle against his shoulder, and saw, through his own muzzle smoke, the big man throw up both his arms, his rifle being flung skyward, and go backwards off his horse. The horse kept on running, sweeping past Longarm and his mules almost before the man hit the ground and went rolling over and over and over.

But there was no time to dwell on the condition of the shot man. The second of the three riders was sweeping down on Longarm. He was the man who had been riding abreast of the coach. His path was almost straight south, bringing him directly at Longarm. Longarm knew he'd better drop the man in a hurry because he was in an ideal position to hit one of his mules. He sighted on the rider when he was still a full three hundred yards away and fired once, levered, fired again, saw the man sag in his saddle and drop his rifle, and held up as the rider tried to stay in the saddle and direct his horse away from Longarm and his mules. Longarm could not chance it. He waited patiently till the man came within fifty yards, and then zeroed in on the man's chest and shot him out of the saddle. It was not the kind of act he was given to, but odds were the man wouldn't have made it anyway, wounded and with no help available out on the big prairie. He swept past the man, who was no more than ten yards away, lying on his side. He could see it was the pudgy man, the one they had called Frank. That meant that the remaining rider was the smallest of the three. It would make him the hardest to hit.

Longarm glanced ahead. He could see that the third man had taken a lesson from what had happened to his two companions. He was riding south, away from the coach, but he was not closing toward Longarm. Instead Longarm heard him fire and saw the smoke and heard the sound of the bullet. The man was firing at his mules. There was no doubt about it. Longarm looked ahead. He was rapidly catching up to the coach. It could not have been more than a half a mile ahead. The wounded mule was still going strong, and neither animal seemed to have been bothered by the gunshots. He saw the man, riding parallel to him, raise up for another shot. With a quick move Longarm reached up with the coach whip in his left hand and slapped the near leader on the left side of his face. The team instantly veered to the right.

145

The riding suddenly got rougher, but it completely took the rider by surprise. He had been shooting from a comfortable distance, and now all of a sudden, his quarry had turned into the hunter and was racing toward him at a fearsome speed. Longarm got his rifle up to his shoulder and waited. He saw the rider wheel his horse and start back toward the coach. It was too long a shot to try to hit the man. The distance was easily three hundred yards. Longarm led the man a trifle and fired. He hoped to hit the man but he knew, more likely, that he was going to hit the horse. He hated it, but there was no choice.

An instant after he fired he saw the horse stumble, but the rider pulled him back up by the reins. Longarm's rifle was empty. Watching the rider, he felt down in the tub until he located the box of cartridges and then rapidly loaded three into the chamber. He cocked the rifle with the lever action and then sighted down on the man, who was now riding away from him. It was a quartering shot, but he had a good piece of the man's back to shoot at. He fired and saw the man slump forward in the saddle. He quickly levered in another cartridge and fired again. This time the horse went down hard, landing almost on his head and rolling over. The man was not flung free.

But Longarm had no time to observe his handiwork. He had to get the mules pointed back north. He figured they'd covered a half mile running almost due east. With his right hand he reached forward with the coach whip and lightly tapped the off leader on the right cheek. The team swerved around to the left, although not quite enough. He pulled on the left reins, and the team swung into the tracks of the coach. He was close enough now that he could see into the interior of the stage even though it was shaded by the canvas covering. Since they'd let him off someone had put down the canvas on both sides. From his distance he peered into the coach, but couldn't make out any figures. He supposed that the doctor was driving the stage. There were no trailing

146

horses to indicate that a fourth man had joined them. He supposed it was the three men who had killed the driver and the guard. Likely they had thought it necessary, though, Longarm thought grimly, they most likely wouldn't have agreed that their own deaths were necessary. He didn't feel so bad about shooting the wounded bandit when he thought of the unnecessary killing of the guard and driver.

He was rapidly overtaking the stage—too rapidly. He saw a wink of light from inside the shaded stage and heard a wind-shattering shot go over his head. Someone from inside was firing at him. He had to assume it was Rita Ann. She was probably shooting at him with his own derringer since, so far as he knew, they did not have a rifle. He immediately swung the team out to the left. The mules pulling the coach were struggling to make it up the grade, barely able to keep a trot. But Longarm's mules, with their light load, paid it scarcely any mind. He kept going left until he was a full hundred yards to the side of the coach. The going was rougher, but it was better than getting a mule shot.

With every step his team was gaining on the coach. Soon he was near enough that he could see a small part of the figure up on the driver's seat. As he had expected it was the doctor. As he drew abreast of the coach, the doctor shot him a frantic look and pulled a revolver out of his pants. With his right hand he fired across his body, snapping off two quick shots. They were well wide, and at such a distance there was little chance of the doctor being able to do much damage with a revolver. But Longarm didn't want to leave even that much to chance. He calculated they didn't have much further to go to the relay station, and he wanted control of the stage before they got there. Regretfully he took up his rifle and aimed toward the stage. He had the pleasure of seeing the doctor throw his arm over his head and duck down.

But Longarm wasn't going to shoot the doctor. Unfortunately, he was necessary to the capture of Carl Lowe. Racing along parallel to the coach Longarm sighted carefully, and shot the near leader in the head. The mule dropped instantly, causing the other nine mules to become entangled in the harness and each other and bringing the stage to an almost immediate stop. Longarm drove on, dropping them a safe distance behind him. He could see mules kicking and rearing in the traces and see the fool of a doctor standing up in the driver's box and lashing at them with the reins as if they were supposed to untangle themselves, get rid of the dead mule, and start up again.

Longarm, using just the reins, was able to circle his team back to his right. He drove a big arc around the stage, watching the doctor, watching the back to see if Rita got out, watching to see if there was anyone on board with a rifle. He knew they had a shotgun because the guard carried one, but he wasn't worried about a shotgun.

And now was to come the hardest part of his trip as he circled behind the stage and commenced to once again come up on the coach's left. He was going to have to bring his team to a stop, and he wasn't sure he altogether knew how to do that. It was going to require some serious cooperation from the mules, and he wasn't sure that such a commodity existed in a mule.

With the mules going in an easy lope, he got hold of the reins and untied them from his gunbelt to have better control, then gradually began to apply backward pressure. To his amazement the mules responded almost as if they weren't half wild and crazy. By the time he came abreast of the stage they were at a slow walk, and with just a little more pressure he brought them to a halt.

After more than two hours of speeding along in the bathtub, the sensation of being motionless was nearly confusing. Most of him still felt like he was moving, though it was plain to his eyes and his senses that he had stopped. He looked off across the desert, through the shimmering heat, at the coach. He calculated it was about a hundred yards away, perhaps a little less. There was no sign of the doctor or Rita Ann, or anyone else for that matter. The mules pulling the stage had quieted down and were simply standing, snarled in the harness, most of them with their heads down, their flanks heaving. His own mules were standing restlessly, stamping a foot now and again and mouthing their bits around. He kept a little back pressure in their mouths to let them know that he was content to be stopped for the time being.

He said in a loud voice, "Doc! Doc! How will you have it?"

There was no answer.

He said again, his voice carrying in the thin, dry air, "Don't be shy, Doc. I'm a man willing to listen to reason. You ain't going anywhere because you can't. Not unless you care to walk. And I'm not going anywhere because I don't want to. Now, you want to talk a little business and see if we can't work out something here? I can wait all day if that is what you have a mind to. Or I can limber up this rifle of mine and start punching holes in that wagon. Maybe I can't see you, but I got plenty of ammunition. Speak up, Doc. Don't be shy."

A moment passed, and then the voice of the doctor came across the distance. He said, "Well, Marshal Long, you are to be congratulated on your reappearance. Rather Lazarus-like, I'd have to say. Quite a conveyance you are transporting yourself in."

"Doc, we can have a good conversation some other time. Right now I want to know what you are ready to do."

He heard the doctor clear his throat. "Ah, what exactly would be my options, Marshal Long?"

Longarm said, "You can surrender right now, or stay out here and die in the sun."

There was a pause. Longarm could barely hear the sound of a whispered conversation. The doctor said, "You don't propose very attractive terms, Marshal. There is a lady present. Why not come over and let us discuss this under more amenable surroundings. I have some brandy here."

"Don't care for it. Look, Doc, I ain't got all day. The sun is getting kind of low in the sky, and I don't want to get caught out here on this freezing-ass desert after dark. Now I know where Carl Lowe is and I'm going to capture him. He may have a few guns protecting him, but that won't make much difference. I'll deal with them just as I dealt with the ones as just left your service. Now, what's it to be?"

"I'm going to have to give this some thought, Marshal. I believe there are other options. I think I still have one or two cards left to play."

"The gold? Hell, you're not going anywhere with that. You've already got one mule down. Before I leave I'll drop a couple more. Won't be any way you can get that team untangled, and even if you could, the ones that are left couldn't pull the load. So what it comes down to is you either decide to surrender to me right now, or figure to die out here in the desert or die trying to walk out. I know the gold ain't going no place, and I got just as easy a time taking Carl Lowe with or without the pair of you. You're out of aces, Doc. Take it or leave it."

"You are making this extremely difficult. There must be a little more give on your part. You are asking for complete and abject surrender."

Longarm picked up his carbine, thumbed the hammer back, aimed and fired a shot through the canvas siding, just high enough so that it would miss anyone sitting down. He heard a screech that sounded very feminine. He said, "You want me to give, I'll give you a few more of these."

The doctor yelled, panic in his voice, "Wait, wait, wait! Hold on a moment, Marshal. All right. Have it your way. Call it a surrender. Whatever you want."

"You giving up?"

"Yes, yes, yes! Of course we are. If you're going to sit out there and shoot us like fish in a barrel, what chance do we have! But let me say it is a disgrace to the federal authority that you serve that you'd bully people in such a fashion."

"Oh, bullshit, Doc. I'm tired of fooling with you. If you surrender, the first thing I want you to do is roll up those canvas sides. Let's get a little light on the interior. See what we got in there."

"But I'll have to come outside to do that."

"You'll be outside soon enough. You might as well tell ol' Rita Ann to get down also. She can be drawing the curtains up on the other side. Just be damn quick about it or I'm going to be obliged to start firing again. My mules are getting restless."

He watched, as impatient as his mules, who were champing their bits and stamping their feet, while the doctor and Rita slowly emerged from the stage and began rolling up the canvas sides. He could see them talking between themselves, but he couldn't hear what they were saying. It took them a good five minutes to get both sides rolled up so he could see into the coach. There could have still been someone lying in the well between the two benches inside, but other than that it appeared empty. The doctor turned and faced him. He said, "Now what is your pleasure, Marshal?"

"I want to see all the guns in that stage laying out this way on the sand. And that includes the weapons you took from the driver and the guard when you killed them."

The doctor said, "I'll not have their deaths on my head! No, sir! Was not me! And it was not Rita either."

Longarm said in disgust, "We can argue out all that later. Right now you let me see them weapons. And take your coat and vest off while you're about it and tell Rita to leave her purse on the ground."

"I take it you're afraid of a lady and an old man."

"You ain't an old man and she damn sure ain't no lady. Now, let's see the firearms and be damn quick about it. You overlook one and you'll be the loser for it. And tell your lady friend there that my derringer had damn well better be in her purse."

The doctor said, "My, my, Marshal. Don't you feel you are taking caution to the extreme? We had a chance to kill you before and didn't. Why should we now?"

"You go ahead and act ignorant if you want to, Doc. Just don't expect me to buy into that particular pot. Now get it done."

He watched with a sense of growing urgency as the doctor went back into the stage and finally emerged. He was carrying three revolvers, a shotgun, and Rita's purse. At Longarm's directions he walked ten yards away from the wagon, toward Longarm, and laid the weapons and the purse on the ground. He straightened up. "Now what would you have us do, Marshal? Search each other? Bind and gag each other?"

The mules were wanting to go. Longarm said, "That ain't such a bad idea, Doc. But right now I want the both of you to walk about a hundred yards south. Just follow the tracks of the stage. Stay apart and keep walking until I tell you to stop."

As soon as they were a distance from the stage, he gingerly let up on the reins and clucked softly to the mules. Half expecting them to bolt, he was pleasantly surprised when they started off slowly, taking one step at a time. He pulled gently on the right rein and the mules came around, heading for the stage. He eased up on the reins a little more and they suddenly wanted to go. It took a great deal of his strength to hold them. He finally got them stopped again, and made the distance over to the stage in a series of stops and starts. The mules were content to walk for a few paces, but after that they figured enough was enough and it was time to run again.

Finally he arrived at the stage. He took a quick look to his right. The doctor and Rita had stopped some distance away in the desert and were watching him intently. They probably didn't understand why he was being so careful with his mules, but he knew. He wasn't sure if he could handle a team of nine mules, the nine still hitched to the stage. Hell, he wasn't sure if he could even get their harness untangled. So the mules he was driving were his only assurance of being able to get off the desert again without walking. He was certain of one thing, and that was he'd walked, and run, across the damned desert for the last time.

With his mules standing at the back of the stage he got carefully out of the bathtub. It was going to be a very tricky moment or two. His legs were a little rubbery from sitting on them so long, but they were just going to have to work for a while longer. He walked carefully beside the near leader, holding the reins, pulling them along the mule's backs, hoping like hell he wouldn't strike a sensitive spot. Finally, moving carefully, he reached the left rear wheel of the stage. The mules were looking walleyed and switching their ears back and forth. He could see the restlessness building in them. As gently as he could he ran the four reins around one of the canopy posts, and quickly tied them off in one big, hard knot. Only then did he take a breath. The mules could kick and squawl, but unless they could pull the wagon and ten other mules, one of them being dead, they weren't going anywhere.

He looked out toward where the doctor and Rita were. The doctor waved, but Rita had sat down. He noticed she was wearing the skirt and blouse she'd worn the day before. It was funny but he hadn't noticed anything about her when they'd first left the stage station. The doctor called, "What now, Marshal? This sun is quite hot."

Longarm said, "Stay where you are. I'll let you know when I'm ready for you."

He walked around to the front of the stage and looked at the mess. The first thing to do was clear the dead mule out of the way. He got out his big clasp knife, stepped in among the harness, and carefully cut the straps that appeared to apply to the near leader. When he was through, the whole mess seemed to have miraculously straightened itself out. The harness was straight and in place. The only problem was that he had reins coming from the off leader, but none from the near leader, because the mule in that position was now one row back. It became clear he would have to take the other mule out of the lead span and rig the next two as leaders. It took him a quarter of an hour, working with his eye and his knife, to finally end up with an eight-mule team and reins running from the two new leaders. The extra mule he simply turned loose. After that he walked toward the end of the stage and waved at the doctor and Rita. "All right. Come on in. Get a move on, I ain't got much time."

While they were trudging toward him, he went quickly to where the doctor had put down the weapons and Rita's purse. He picked up the lot and loaded them in the bathtub, taking time to open Rita's purse and see that his derringer was indeed inside. He took up his gun-belt and strapped it on, and then rammed his Colt revolver home in the holster. It felt good, it felt right, it felt complete again. He took the derringer and broke it open. One cartridge had been fired. He reckoned that was the little wink he'd seen from the darkness of the interior of the stage when he'd been traveling right behind them. Fortunately the shot had missed, but that would have been something if the shot had gone home into one of his mules and pulled him up dead in the ground. Stopped by a woman firing his own derringer!

He closed the derringer and slipped it under the clip in his big buckle. He had spare ammunition for it, but it was in his saddlebags and they were still on top of the stage. Meanwhile he had more important business to attend to. He took the bottle of whiskey out of the tub and set it inside the stage as the doctor and Rita came up. He said, "Hold up. I want to make sure you ain't carrying anything besides bad intentions."

He searched them both very thoroughly, even making Rita raise up her dress so he could feel about in her underwear for any concealed weapons. All during the search she kept up a steady stream of abuse, to which he paid not the slightest bit of attention. When he was satisfied they were clean, he motioned toward the coach.

"All right. Get on in there. It's time we had a little conversation."

The doctor went to the back and sat in the right rear corner. Rita sat a little down from him toward the rear. Longarm sat almost where he had before they'd put him off. He had the bottle of whiskey between his feet, and he took it up and pulled the cork home and had a long swallow. When he was through, he rammed the cork and set the bottle on the bench beside him. He made no offer of a drink to the others. "Now then," he said, talking to both of them, "let's get down to the business at hand. I'm going to want to know who is waiting at that relay station and just who they are and what kind of gunhands they will be. I'm going to want to know what they are expecting to show up and when. Now I need this information and I intend to get it. I don't have a lot of time, so you can expect me to be pretty quick at getting down to ways to make you tell me what I want to know. I also want to know if ya'll intend to cooperate at all. I don't have to tell you it will make it easier on you if you do. But just remember, I have already got this particular business figured out and you can't save this scheme. It's already finished. And I will have Carl Lowe back in prison. You can depend on that. Now who wants to start talking first?"

He glanced at the doctor and then he glanced at Rita. Neither said anything. Rita was staring out at the desert; the doctor had a pleasant smile on his face. As Longarm looked at him directly, the doctor smiled broadly and said, "Looks like it is going to be a particularly beautiful sunset."

Longarm nodded. "All right, if that is the way you'll have it." He looked from Rita to the doctor and back to Rita. To the doctor he said, pointing at Rita, "Now I already know she is about as tough as a hoe handle, so I can't afford to waste a lot of time on her. But Doc, I got you figured for a man with lace on his underwear. I figure you'll tell me what I need to know the quickest.

So you just get up and make your way down to this end of the coach, and me and you will get outside where I'll have more room to work. Don't make me come get you. That would just embarrass you worse. So get up and come along."

The doctor nodded. "As you say." He stood up, and was starting to walk toward the end of the coach when Rita suddenly put up her hand as if to shove him back. She said to Longarm, "Wait!"

Longarm was about to stand. He eased back on the bench. The doctor had been walking forward, stooping a little under the canvas top. Longarm realized again that the man seemed to get bigger each time he saw him. He looked at Rita. "You got something to say?"

She was talking to Longarm, but she looked at the doctor. She said, "You got it all wrong. You could pull off his fingers one by one and he'd never do anything but smile. You don't know who you are dealing with here."

The doctor said, "Rita, please, dear. Don't talk anymore."

She said to the doctor, "Anson, I have to. I couldn't stand to see you hurt." She turned to Longarm with almost a triumphant air. "You are wrong, Mr. Marshal Longarm. This man is tougher than you are. He can stand anything. You could roast him over a fire and he'd never tell you anything." Her voice broke just perceptibly. "But I couldn't take it. I wouldn't be able to stand to see him hurt."

"All right," Longarm said. "I don't care how I get it. Sit down, Doc. The lady will do the talking."

Rita said proudly, "He's not a doctor. He's an actor. One of the finest actors in the country."

Longarm glanced back and forth between them. "Yeah? Who does he act with, John Wilkes Booth?"

She flared up. "You make jokes! You don't understand what a great man he is. He had one of the finest acting troupes in California. He was the toast of San

Francisco. I should know. I've been with him for five years.''

Longarm said, "He's such a great actor, how come he took up stage-robbing? Wasn't drawing much at the gate?''

"He's a genius!'' she said proudly. "His mind is restless. He has to be constantly challenging himself. Look at what he did back at the relay station. For three days he played the part of a drunken, shriveled-up, ruined man. He looked small, he acted small. And yet he is physically the strongest man I've ever known.''

Longarm looked down the coach. "Yeah, how about that, Doc? Or Anson, or whatever it is. You look all different now. How'd you do that?''

The man said with a small smile, "That would be something it takes years to learn, Marshal. Right now I am concerned with Rita talking too much. You'd spoil everything if you did that, dear. I know it looks black right now, but one never knows what prospects might emerge from the dim gloom.''

She said, pointing at Longarm, "Anson, you don't know this man. He is mean as anything. You already know how he hurt Frank and Wayne and Potts. And I told you how he treated me that second night. Like I was nothing but a piece of meat!''

Longarm said, "Thought you might like to know how it felt. At least I didn't steal your derringer while I was at it.''

She gave Longarm a fierce glance. "You are a savage. And I cannot allow you to hurt this man, this great actor.''

Longarm laughed slightly. He said, "You ain't so bad yourself. You fooled the hell out of me, I'll give you that.''

Anson said, "Rita, I prefer you not to say anything.''

Longarm turned and looked at him. He said, "Anson, you sit back down there. Let's let the lady talk. Otherwise we are going out of the wagon and I damn well may see how many fingers I have to pull off before you tell me what you know.''

Anson said, ''I never have complimented you on your manner of conveyance. I have been chased before, but never by a man riding in a mule-drawn bathtub. Very ingenious. It also means I wasted my time with those miserable Mexicans finding out everything I could about that station. I was assured by them there were no vehicles of any kind you could use to chase us. Most inventive.''

''Let's get on with it,'' Longarm said. ''I'm in a hurry.'' He turned to Rita. ''Who is at that station? How many are waiting for you two?''

Instead of answering she looked at the actor. ''Anson? Please?''

He shook his head and folded his arms. ''I'd rather you didn't, my dear. I have not yet given up hope. The game is still afoot. I don't mind the pain and I think I can hold out until well after dark. By then help might well arrive when they realize we could have had trouble.''

She said, talking in front of Longarm as if he didn't exist, ''I'm not sure it would work. You should have seen him when he beat the hell out of Wayne and them. And you just saw how he can shoot. Anson, I'm afraid we have to cooperate. Perhaps he'll make us a deal, let us go.'' She turned to Longarm. ''Marshal, if we help you get what you want will you be fair with us? Will you turn your head long enough for us to get away?''

Anson said instantly, ''You can't bargain with the devil, Rita. No, don't expect any mercy from him.''

Longarm said, ''You might be surprised, Mr. Actor, what I might be willing to do. It's Carl Lowe I am after. I calculate it was you got the party together and bore the expense to break him out of prison. That right?''

Anson nodded his head modestly. ''I think I could say with some degree of fairness that I engineered most of the plot, though I did not finance the project with my own money. Others were involved. By the way, as a sop to your ego, Carl warned us about you from the beginning. He said you had to be thrown off the scent. He appears to fear you more than the rest of the law put together.''

Rita said eagerly, "What will you do for us, Longarm, if we assist you in capturing Carl Lowe?''

Longarm shook his head. "I can't get over the way you talk so different than you did back at the station. And what you and I did . . . I mean, was that part of it?''

The actor suddenly laughed. He said, "Don't disconcert yourself, Marshal. I can assure you that Rita was not *acting* that part, if I understand you correctly.''

Longarm said to both of them, making his voice firm and earnest, "Look, I got no real interest in the two of you. Carl Lowe is who I want. It looks bad I let him get away from me out there on the desert. You play straight with me and I don't see any reason why either one of you has to get hurt. In fact I'll guarantee it.''

Rita looked down the coach at the actor. "Anson? I heard he is a man of his word. They say he is mean as hell, but he keeps his word.''

Anson studied Longarm's face for a moment. "You propose a deal of some sort, Marshal?''

Longarm studied the man. He had discarded the glasses and his face looked much younger, firmer. And without the tight-fitting coat and vest he was a good deal more broad-shouldered and broad-chested than he had appeared. "I'm after Carl Lowe. I've said there is no need for you or Rita to get hurt in the deal, not unless you cause trouble. But I got to know one thing first. Who shot the driver and the guard?''

"That," Rita said quickly, "was Wayne's work. And Frank's. They never even give them men a chance to surrender. Rode up and blazed away. Next thing we had two dead men riding in the driver's box on a runaway coach. Frank and Wayne got it stopped, and then Anson did the driving from then on.''

Longarm looked down toward the actor. "You handled that team pretty good, Anson. Where'd you learn that?''

Anson smiled smugly. "I once served as the coach-man for a rich family in Saint Louis. Drove a four-in-hand."

"What'd you do that for? No acting jobs available?"

Anson chuckled. "It was the best way to learn the layout of their house and their comings and goings. It was where I met Rita. She did the robbery while I was driving the Mister and Madame around." He laughed briefly.

"And you didn't have anything to do with killing that guard and driver?"

Anson shook his head emphatically. "That is not my style. I do not care for bloodshed at all. Only if it is necessary. Absolutely necessary."

"Then I reckon we can deal."

Anson glanced at Rita and then at Longarm. "What are you saying?"

"I'm saying you help me capture or kill whoever is waiting at that station, and as far as *I'm* concerned you can write your own ticket."

Anson looked at him hard. "You will let us go?"

"I'm saying I don't care what you do or where you go. You need it any plainer than that?"

Rita said, "They say he keeps his word. They say he's tough as hell, but fair."

Anson said, "Yes, I know." He pondered for a moment, and then shrugged. "I guess that means we have to pass on the gold. Is that right, Marshal?"

Longarm laughed lightly. "I think we got to draw the line somewhere."

Anson sighed. "Dammit, I invested a lot of time and not a little money in this venture."

Rita said, "But we can start all over again, Anson. We'll be free. The plan is ruined anyway."

Longarm said, "That's enough talk. What's it to be?"

Chapter 10

Rita said, "Besides Carl, there are only two men there. There would have been five, not counting Anson and Carl, but you killed the other three. They were to have ridden out, taken control of the coach, and put the driver and guard afoot." She looked down. "You saw where it went wrong."

From the front of the coach Anson said, "And I can tell you who made it go wrong."

"Yeah? Who?"

"Never mind for now. Go ahead, Rita."

"Anyway, that's all that is at that station. We were suppose to arrive there early this evening, switch the gold to a special wagon that has been built, and then head south for Mexico. We figured to have at least a two-day head start, and did not believe anyone could find us. And if they did, we would have enough guns to fight them off. Of course we would have had more if so many of the damn fools who broke Carl out hadn't gotten themselves killed or captured."

Longarm said, "The two at the relay station . . . gunmen?"

"One is for certain." She looked up the coach to Anson. "What should I say about the other?"

161

Anson laughed shortly. "He's someone whose name you will know, Marshal. You decide if he's a gunman. Riley Hanks."

Longarm blinked in spite of himself. It was a name well known to him. Riley Hanks had been suspected of planning and benefiting from the robbery of his own bank in Tucson. Nothing had ever been proved against him, but he had been shut down by territorial and federal officers. That had been three years past. In the intervening time he was thought to have been involved, usually behind the scenes, in several bank and several train robberies. He had been a particularly elusive fugitive because he was seldom a part of the actual robbery itself. But yes, Longarm thought, you could call the man a gunman. He was tough and smart and utterly ruthless. He turned to Anson. "I see what you mean about who made it go wrong. Hanks wanted the driver and guard killed. Yeah, he likes blood. Being a businessman was too tame for him."

For some time Longarm had been watching one of the horses—he thought it was the animal the big man had been riding—slowly working his way toward the stage. Now the horse was only about a hundred yards away, standing, his reins drooping to the ground, staring at the coach and the mules. He obviously wanted company. He'd wandered around and smelled the dead horse and smelled the dead men. It was clear he wanted to come in where there might be feed and water. The desert was still fearfully hot, and Longarm reckoned the horse hadn't had a drink in some time. He knew there was a barrel of water strapped to the side of the coach along with a fair-sized bucket. He said to Rita, "I don't know if you are as good with horses as you are with men, but I want you to dip up a bucket of water out of that barrel and go out and fetch that horse in. Don't try and ride him. I will be standing here with a Winchester and you are well within range. So don't look at it as an opportunity to escape. Just go fetch the horse."

The actor said, "I protest, sir. That is not proper work

for a woman. If the horse must be had, let me go."

Longarm shook his head. "You set right still, Mister Anson. I like you in close view." He said to Rita, "Get moving. Just take the bridle and lead him in. If he smells the water he'd likely come to you. Let him have a drink."

They both watched as she walked across the desert carrying the gallon bucket. She carried it lightly as if it were no burden at all. Longarm had gotten down and gone to the bathtub to fetch his rifle in case she got any ideas. Anson said, "You wouldn't actually shoot a woman, would you, Marshal?"

"She's not a woman right now. She's a prisoner."

The man sounded amused. "But if you are planning on letting us go, why would you care if she took French leave now?"

Longarm looked around at the coach where Anson was sitting. He said, "You better get out and go take a look at the team you'll be driving. You will be short two mules and I had to do some guesswork on the harness."

"I'm to be driving?"

"Of course. Wouldn't you have driven in if things had gone according to plan?"

Anson came down from the coach. "I'm not sure. I suppose so."

They both watched as the horse nickered, catching scent of the water, and came trotting toward Rita. He came up to her and she let him drink out of the bucket while she patted his head. Anson said, "A most remarkable woman."

"She's something else, all right. Just what I'm not sure." He glanced at the man. "She told you what she and I did. It doesn't make you jealous?"

Anson shook his head. "Rita has her own tastes. I don't try and control them anymore than she tries to control mine."

Longarm said, "You better get up in the driver's box and get ready. Here she comes." As the man turned away Longarm said, "I don't guess I have to warn you, do I?"

Anson turned around and smiled. "Not to give you away? I think I understand you well enough to know that I would be the first one killed."

"And Rita. Probably at the same time."

Anson nodded. "I think we understand each other."

"Good," Longarm said evenly. "Was I you, I'd make this one of my better performances, Doc."

Longarm waited until Rita came up with the saddle horse. The animal looked to be in good condition. Longarm wanted him just in case he needed to get off on his own in a hurry. He checked the horse's girth, let him have some more water, and then tied him to the end of the coach away from the mules. His last task was to go to the bathtub, find the box of cartridges, and reload his rifle and check the loads in his revolver. Finally he climbed up in the back of the stage and yelled to Anson to move out. After a moment he felt the stage creak and then start forward. It was a far cry from the jolting beginning that had begun the trip back at the relay station. Rita had gone up to the very end of the coach, and was huddled in a corner against the wooden box that held the safe. Longarm made no attempt to speak to her.

He got out his watch and looked at it. It was just seven-thirty. The sun was already beginning to flatten itself against the far horizon. Longarm desperately wanted to reach the relay station with a little light left. He was not sure of what to expect, in spite of what Anson and Rita had said, and he needed light for the work ahead. He said to Rita, "What condition are the relay stationkeeper and his mule hustlers likely to be in?"

She said in a dull voice, "You figure it out. You know the kind of man you are dealing with. I begged Anson not to get involved with Hanks. Didn't do any good."

Longarm didn't say anything. Instead he looked out the side of the coach at the desert that seemed to be moving by with agonizing slowness. Either the mules were having a hard time with the grade, or the actor was taking his own time for his own reasons. Longarm stuck his head and shoulders out the side of the coach and yelled forward. "Get them damn mules moving, Doc, or all deals are off. Slap the reins on their backs!"

After that they seemed to go a little faster. Longarm did not think the station would be much further. He made no attempt to conceive any sort of plan since he didn't have the slightest idea what might be waiting for him. About all he had resolved was that his call for surrender would almost instantly be followed by a bullet. He did not believe that he was dealing with anyone that could be trusted, and that included the two in the coach with him.

At the rear of the coach the saddle horse and the mule team pulling the bathtub were following along docilely, although Longarm thought he detected a look of mutiny in the eyes of his mules. For himself, he was tired and irritated and burning with a slow, hot anger. This was one job he was ready to be finished with. But he intended to make certain he finished the people who had caused it. If things went his way, Carl Lowe was going to wish he'd never left his prison cell and Riley Hanks would gladly give a fortune just to clerk in a bank again.

The stage slowly creaked to a halt. Longarm heard Anson calling his name. He jumped out the back, carrying his rifle, and mindful of the heels of his mules, went around to the front of the coach and looked up at the driver's box. Anson motioned. "There it is."

They had reached the top of the grade. Down a gentle slope, perhaps a half a mile away, were a cluster of small buildings. It wasn't as big a place as the Higginses' station. Longarm counted only two outbuildings beside the main one, which he reckoned to be the station. He could see a couple of corrals crowded with what he took to be mules, but it appeared that, back of the main building, were two or three horses. The distance was too great to be certain.

165

Anson said, "I am at your order, oh, captain, my captain." He gave a mocking smile. "A little poetry for the occasion."

Longarm looked up at him, considering. If the man chose to go counter to what Longarm instructed, he'd be signing his own death warrant, but he would also be putting Longarm in a bind. He said, "Doc, you planning on carrying through on this, or do you want to get shot?"

The actor laughed. "You seem to require some convincing, Marshal. Give me your orders. I'll carry them out."

Longarm said, "I want you to point this team of mules right at that station and I want you to get them moving. When we are about a couple of hundred yards from the place I want you to whomp 'em up as fast as they can go."

"I may not be able to stop them."

"Oh, you'll stop them all right," Longarm said. "I'm going to get you some help. But just point them straight at the front door of the station and I guarantee you they will stop. Now whip them up."

As the stage began to move, Longarm hopped up on the right side, crouching on the water barrel which was just back of the driver's box. He said, loud enough for Anson to hear, "I'm right here, Doc. Keep that in mind."

They were moving. The mules, through some frantic strength that only mules knew how to summon, were digging in and pulling the heavy load down the slope at a trot and trying to stretch it to a lope. In the open coach Longarm could crane his head around and just catch sight of the station. It was coming closer and closer as the mules picked up speed.

Now they had come off the slope and were on a flat piece of prairie that would run to the front of the station. Looking from the coach was no help since the station was more ahead of them than toward the side. With the coach jouncing and rumbling along, Longarm cautiously stood up on the water barrel, clutching the overhead luggage rack with his left hand, and looked over the top of the stage. He figured they were within a hundred yards of the station. He watched the distance, gauging his timing, and then began yelling. He said in a loud voice, "HELP! HELP! I CAN'T STOP! HELP! HEAD THESE MULES!"

He saw Anson glance back at him in annoyance. Longarm said to him, "Start pulling up, you damn fool!"

Below him he saw the brake go on against the front wheel, and saw Anson set back against the reins. The mules were slowing, but they were still traveling at a clip a little faster than a trot and the station was scarcely fifty yards away. As he watched, Longarm saw three men come running out of the front of the station. One he instantly recognized as Carl Lowe, and another he thought was Riley Hanks. The third he didn't recognize personally, but he recognized the type. The man was there for his gun. All three men came running toward the stage, grabbing the lead mules by the head and slowing them down. By the time they got into the station yard the mules were walking and about to stop. Longarm had ducked down when the men had neared, and now he dropped off the stage as it came to a halt. He drew his revolver, cocking it, and walked around the end of the coach. The three men were standing just back from the lead mules. As he walked toward them they stepped further away from the mules, backing toward the station. They had not seen him. The gunman was the first in the line, Carl Lowe was second and a little back, and Riley Hanks was at the far end. The light was starting to fail, but the men stood out in clear outline against the lighter stone of the relay station. Longarm was about five yards away, but they had not glanced his way. Riley Hanks seemed to be looking up at the driver's box, saying something to the actor. Longarm had his revolver down by his side. He stopped and said sharply, "Hold it! Hands up!"

As he had expected, the gunman was the first to react. He immediately wheeled toward Longarm, his hand going for his pistol. Longarm brought up his revolver and fired, catching the man at the top of the chest. He was aware of the man staggering backwards and of Carl Lowe immediately dropping to the ground and covering his head with his hands, but his attention was on Riley Hanks. Hanks was a big man with a white linen duster over a good suit of clothes. He had gotten his hand under the duster and was starting to draw his weapon when Longarm came around on him. Longarm said, "Hold it! You're under arrest!"

But then the linen duster flared out as Riley Hanks finished his draw. Longarm fired, hitting the man in the left side of the chest. He saw the sudden crimson stain on the white of the duster. But Hanks didn't fall. He was a big man, stout, with heavy shoulders and a big girth. He took a step forward, struggling to bring his gun up. Longarm aimed carefully and shot him two inches under the left collarbone. He flopped over backwards, the pistol falling from his lifeless fingers.

It was all over. Longarm felt suddenly tired. It seemed the chase had gone on for months or years. He walked slowly forward, his revolver at the ready. It was clear that Hanks was finished, but Longarm wasn't so sure about the gunman. He walked to where the man lay sprawled in the dust. There was blood coming out of his nose and mouth. Longarm could see his slug had taken the man just above the heart. He'd gone down dead.

But there was still Carl Lowe cowering on the ground. Longarm said tiredly, "Get up, Carl. It's all over. Get up, dammit!"

His attention was solely on the locksmith cowering on the ground when he was suddenly hit from behind and above by a blow that knocked him flat on his face on the ground and sent his revolver spinning out of his hand. For an instant the power of the attack had stunned him so that he wasn't sure what was happening. Then he realized that someone had his arms wrapped around his neck and was pulling his head back, trying to snap it. Whoever it was was sitting astride him in such a way that he couldn't rise or twist his body. He tried grabbing at the forearms that were clutched around his neck, but it took him only an instant to realize he would not be able to pry them loose that way. Whoever had him was incredibly strong. And then Longarm remembered what Rita had said about Anson's strength. It was clear that the man had leapt out of the driver's box, landing on Longarm's back and driving him to the ground. He could hear Anson making little grunting sounds as he twisted and pulled at Longarm's head.

For a few seconds Longarm tried to strike backwards with his elbows, but his foe was too well positioned for him to get in a solid hit. But he was going to have to do something quick. Anson had pulled his head back so far that his back was swayed and his chest was completely off the ground. When there was no more give that way, then his neck would have to break. He could feel a vague grayness behind his eyes, and he realized he was being suffocated. And to make matters worse, he saw Carl Lowe raise his head and look at the pistol that had flown out of Longarm's hand and fallen very near him.

In desperation Longarm managed to get his hand down inside his belt buckle. He could just touch the derringer with his fingers, but he couldn't quite reach it because of the way the actor was pulling him back. With all his strength, and knowing it would choke him more, he forced his head down. In one swift instant he was able to grab the little gun. He knew there wasn't but one shot in it and he couldn't miss. As Anson pulled him back up again, bending him almost backwards at the waist, Longarm reached across his own chest, curved the gun under his left arm until it was pointing upward and backward, and fired.

He heard a woman scream, but most importantly he felt the arms loosen around his neck. He sucked air into his lungs and gave a hard roll to his left. He felt the weight of the actor leave him. Gasping, he struggled to his hands and knees and then, slowly, stood up. Carl Lowe had almost crawled to within reach of Longarm's revolver. Longarm took two steps and kicked the man hard under the chin. The little locksmith rose up in the air and then settled back, his arms outflung, his body limp.

The screaming went on, but Longarm was conscious only of Rita in the coach and the guns he had in the bathtub. He made his way past the mules and then sat down on the side of the tub, still gasping. All of a sudden Rita jumped out of the back of the stage and ran to where Anson was lying. She knelt down beside him, rubbing his face with her hands and kissing him feverishly. He didn't move. She turned and screamed at Longarm, "You've killed him, you bastard! You've killed him!"

It came out a croak, but it came out. Longarm said, "Guess that was his last role. He didn't do it too good."

His strength was coming back, but he was still unsure of his footing as he made it to the back of the stage and hunted up the bottle of whiskey he'd left there. He took down two good swallows and then corked the bottle. There was still a lot of work to be done before he could rest. He walked out from the stage. Carl Lowe was sitting up, shaking his head. Rita had walked away from Anson's body and was hugging herself and crying. Longarm said, "Carl, get the hell up. And you too, Rita Ann. These mules have got to get unhitched and put away. So put your cares and woes aside and get over here and help."

Chapter 11

That first night, after a little something to eat and drink, all he could do was bind both of them hand and foot. Lowe he bound with leather thongs, his hands behind his back. He knew the man could open safes, and he might also be able to open knots. He tied up Rita with less severity, allowing her to have her hands in front of her. The only leather he used on her was around her ankles when he secured her to a post in the common room of the station. Through it all Rita had been stoic and silent, not having spoken a word to him since he'd killed Anson. Lowe had been submissive and frightened. He seemed grateful that all Longarm was going to do was tie him up in an extremely uncomfortable position for the entire night. Longarm had made it clear from the first that he wasn't fond of either one of them and the less trouble they gave him the easier they would find life.

It had taken half the night, but they'd finally managed to get all the mules unhitched, the bathtub mules as well, and into the corral for water and hay. Longarm had turned the four saddle horses, the one he'd brought and the three the men who'd ridden to the station had brought, in with the mules. It had caused some kicking and squealing among the mules, but they had gradually settled down and accepted the horses.

There was nothing he could do about the bodies. Rita had slipped out while they were making a kind of supper and put a blanket over Anson, but nothing else had been done. As best he could figure, it the next stage was not due until about thirty-six hours after they had arrived. Until that stage came, or somebody showed up who knew how to work a telegraph, there was really nothing he could do. He knew that he was not up to the task of harnessing a team of mules that could pull the stage, and he had no intention of breaking his fingers trying.

But he had to figure some way to handle his prisoners. He didn't want to watch them every moment, and there were firearms and horses all about. There was no good place to lock them up, either together or separately, and he wasn't sure there was a lock on the place that would hold Carl Lowe. In the end he gathered up all the ammunition from all the firearms, and there were quite a few, and took it out in the desert and hid it. He did the same with all but one of the bridles and saddles for the horses. He didn't figure either Carl Lowe or Rita could ride a horse without either one of those necessary articles.

But by noon of the next day he had discovered the bodies of the stationkeeper, who had been a bachelor, and the two mule hustlers who had worked for him. Longarm put Carl Lowe to work with a shovel and pick burying them in individual graves. After that he felt the necessity of doing something about the three bodies lying in front of the station. He saddled the best of the horses, led him around to the front, and got a rope around Riley Hanks and the gunmen. Then he mounted up and dragged them a mile or two out in the desert, and left them for the coyotes and the buzzards. He took the identification from both men, noting that Hanks had been carrying almost a thousand dollars in cash. That was probably intended for use on their trip to Mexico with the gold.

When he returned, he gave Rita the choice of taking a shovel and burying Anson. When she just folded her arms and walked away, he roped the actor's ankles together and dragged him off to join his collaborators.

After that he put the horse away and hid the bridle in a stack of hay. There was a small, stout wagon parked at the back of the station, and Longarm asked Rita if that had been the vehicle they had intended to transport the gold to Mexico in. She refused to answer him. He said, "You were all suckers, you just didn't know it. And that includes that actor fellow you were so fond of. At least I got some respect for him. Once Riley Hanks got his hands on that gold you were all dead anyway. Riley Hanks, or any of his kind, don't share. So you ain't lost nothing."

She rounded on him. "That's all you know! Anson had it all figured. It would have been Riley and his gunmen who would have perished. *We'd* have been the ones took the gold to Mexico."

He laughed. "How the hell were you and Doc going to do away with four gunmen, figuring that I wouldn't have killed three of them for you, and Riley Hanks and Carl Lowe?"

"Poison," she said. "Their first meal here would have been their last."

Longarm shook his head. "You two were a pair of sweethearts, weren't you. Remind me to keep you out of the kitchen."

She put on a pout. "Don't worry. Doc threw away the poison when you captured us. He knew the game was up."

"He damn sure didn't go out like it." He rubbed his neck. "Strong sonofabitch. Like to have broke my head off."

"Yes, and you had to shoot him. Like a coward!"

Longarm shook his head and walked out to check on Carl. He stood, watching the plodding, methodical way

173

the man worked. Carl Lowe was fairly small, fairly ordinary-looking, and completely indistinguishable from any one of a thousand men. Longarm realized that he could stare at Carl's face for fifteen minutes and then look away and not be able to give an accurate description of the man.

Carl was more than willing to talk about the robbery and how it had come about. He seemed very anxious to please Longarm. Longarm thought he'd always been anxious to please anyone with power over him. Carl said that the original idea had been Anson's. His real name was Anson Burke and he really hadn't been that much of an actor. Carl gave a shy smile. "He was good, all right, you understand, but he preferred other ways to gettin' his supper. He liked to make fools out of folks and he figured the best way to do that was steal their money. Anson wasn't a man cared much for folks. Thought he was a good deal superior."

It had been Anson, whom Carl had worked with before, who had reached him in prison with word about the gold shipments. Carl had gotten word back that he'd be more than glad to help if he could be broken out. But money had been a problem. Carl had recommended that Anson hook up with Riley Hanks. He knew the man had money and he knew he'd bankroll a job if the payoff was big enough.

Carl said cheerfully, "My cut was to be a quarter of the take, plus bein' broke out of prison. Anson and Riley was gonna split the balance after expenses. Them gunhands was just that, hired gunhands. They didn't get no split." Carl shook his head. "But I'll tell you, Marshal, soon as I figured it was you on my tail, I knowed we didn't have much chance. Minute I heard you yesterday evenin' call on us to get our hands up I knowed the dance was over. I just went for the dirt and hoped you'd shoot high."

Longarm knew that Rita believed he was not going to arrest her. He knew she believed it because she thought he had given her and Anson his word that if they cooperated with him they could write their own ticket. He knew she fully expected to go back to civilization as a free woman at the first opportunity. When he'd been tying her up the night before she'd asked why. He'd answered that he'd killed her lover and he always made it a point to tie up the girlfriends of the lovers he'd killed, especially when he was sleeping under the same roof with them. She had seemed to accept that readily enough.

The station was not a meal stop for passengers. As a consequence it was much smaller than Higgins's station. The common room was half the size of Higgins's, and there was no bar, makeshift or not. The stationkeeper lived in just one windowless room. The bathroom was anyplace you cared to go outdoors. There was a kind of kitchen, but it had just a small, wood-burning stove and a big washtub for the dishes and the pots. There was no inside water, just a pump outside the back door of the common room. The first night Longarm had left Carl and Rita tied up in the common room. He'd slept in the stationkeeper's quarters, blocking the door with a chair. As tired as he had been, one of the prisoners could have gotten loose, sneaked in, and cut his throat and he would have never woken up.

The telegraph key sat on a table in the stationkeeper's quarters. Longarm looked at it from time to time, but it was just a piece of metal as far as he was concerned. Of no more use than an empty gun.

The second evening he fried up a batch of bacon and opened some cans of tomatoes. There were some stale biscuits, and he appropriated several. He was sitting eating at the small table in the common room when Rita came up and stood behind him. She rested her hand lightly on his shoulder. He ignored her presence. She said, "I ain't mad at you no more."

He took a quick glance over his shoulder at her face. She was smiling down at him with that crooked little smile she used. He said, "That's good. I don't like folks to be mad at me."

She began rubbing her hand along his neck, and then slipped it inside his shirt and ran her fingers through the curly hair on his chest. She said, "You feel all nice and warm. But I bet I could get you a lot warmer."

He put his fork down and sat still. In a moment she came around his chair and leaned down with her face close to his. She let her tongue come out and ran it along her lips. "You remember this?"

He started laughing, he couldn't help himself. He said, "Rita, I got to hand it to you, you are some piece of work. Old Anson's bones ain't even picked clean by the buzzards and you are already saddling your next horse. Woman, you just go whichever way the wind is blowing, don't you?"

She straightened up. "Well, I don't see where you got any right to get on your high and mighty. You liked it well enough before."

He said, looking up at her, "Yeah, but that was before I knew where it had been. No thanks, miss, I don't reckon I'll have any more of your pie. The first few pieces didn't altogether agree with me."

As she stalked off, Carl Lowe came to the table with a small skillet full of bacon and beans accompanied by a hunk of stale bread and a pitcher of water. He set to work eating the beans. As he shoveled in the food he said, "This is mighty good, Marshal. A man learns to appreciate the good things when he's done without."

Longarm had announced that he would not be cooking for anyone else, and after hearing Rita talk about poison, he was not about to let her near the food. As a consequence he had said that everyone was on their own so far as vittles went. "Eat what you can find."

But while he was frying bacon it had seemed just as simple to fry up some extra, and Carl Lowe had taken advantage of it. Longarm had come to feel friendly toward the little man. He seemed so innocuous, so innocent, it was hard to believe he was a robber and a thief.

176

Longarm said, "Carl, I hate like hell to bind you hand and foot like I done last night."

Carl paused with his spoon in the air. "I don't mind, Marshal. I know you got to do your job."

"I got the bridles and saddles hidden away, but as good a horseman as you appear to be, you might mount one of those animals out there and use a piece of rope for a bridle and make a clean getaway."

Carl stared at him blankly. "Horseman? What gives you the idea I'm any kind of horseman, Marshal? I don't know much about horses. I'm city-bred."

Longarm said, "Hell, Carl, I saw you break off from the main bunch and head north. I read your sign. You were pulling a packhorse. I damn near got within rifle range of you before my horse broke a leg."

Carl chuckled. "Marshal, that there is good one on you. That wasn't me a-horseback. And they wasn't no packhorse. I was the pack on the horse. That was Johnny Jimbuck, one of the prisoners as broke out with me. His job was to get me loose and up to Buckeye. To meet Mr. Hanks."

"Johnny Jimbuck?"

"Yessir. He is a Comanche Indian. They say he could ride a wildcat without a saddle if you could grow one big enough." He took a bite of beans. "So he wuz the one got me out." He chuckled. "I 'ppreciate the compliment, Marshal, but I was hangin' on was all I was doin'."

Longarm said, "Well, if I took into account all the bother you've caused me, Carl, I'd take you out and hang you to a tree. Save me the trouble of taking you back to prison."

Carl chuckled. "Ain't no trees around here, Marshal. Besides, me and you is professionals. I reckon the trouble I caused you you just chalked up to a day's work. And I don't mind so much going back to prison. The warden there give me a good job and I got treated pretty good. Didn't have to work out in all that heat breakin' rocks."

"What were you doing?"

Carl swallowed and tore off a piece of bread. "I worked on the locks and the keys. They was always gettin' broke. The warden had me a little workshop set up with a steam-powered metal lathe. Wasn't all that bad."

Longarm laughed. When he could stop he said, "You telling me the warden turned you loose on the locks and the keys?"

Carl looked sheepish. "Yeah. I reckon I kind of took advantage of the situation."

"That how you broke yourself and the others out?"

Carl Lowe blushed and put his head down. "Yeah, I reckon."

A little later, when they were having coffee, Carl said, "You know, Marshal, I reckon it's right that I'm going back to Yuma." He looked down. "I been gettin' tired of all this robbery. I didn't mind openin' the safes, you understand, but they always seemed to be killing and hard stuff went with it. I don't like all that hard stuff. Fact is, I don't like guns. Scared me to death all them guns goin' off yesterday when you showed up."

Longarm gave him a glance. "Looked to me like you were trying to get your hands on mine."

Carl Lowe nodded. "Yessir. And I know you ain't never goin' to believe me, but I was gettin' your gun to make that feller let go of your neck before he hurt you bad."

Longarm stared at him for a long moment. Strangely enough, he did believe him. He finally said, "Well, I thank you for the thought, Carl. I reckon I'm sorry I kicked you in the chin."

Carl Lowe reached up and rubbed his bruised chin. "Wasn't the worst lick I ever got." He sighed. "And probably won't be the last. Reckon that stage will get here tomorrow?"

Longarm shrugged. "According to the way I calculate

it. Ought to be in here early morning. At least I hope so.''

"But it will be southbound."

Longarm said dryly, ''We'll find a way to turn it around. Trust me on that.''

That night he took Carl into the stationkeeper's quarters to sleep. When he was blocking the door with a chair under the knob Carl Lowe said, ''Marshal, if you are aimin' to keep me in with that chair agin the door, you got it on the wrong side.''

"It's to keep her out," Longarm said.

"You ain't scairt of that nice lady, are you?"

Longarm looked at him grimly. ''Yes.''

"Why, I think she is just a sweetheart."

"You didn't shoot her lover and you ain't standing in her way."

He tied Carl's hands in front of him with leather thongs. ''Now, Carl, I'm gonna kind of loose-tie you tonight. Don't get loose and make me chase you across that damn desert, Carl. I am *sick* of that desert. You understand? Sick of it.''

"Yessir," Carl said. ''You can go ahead and rest easy. Ain't no way out of here for me. Nowhere to go. Besides, these here leather knots ain't like regular ones.''

"Good," Longarm said. But just as a safeguard, once he was ready for bed, he tied a long thong around Carl's hands and then tied it to his own ankle. Carl slept on the floor. Longarm took the bed, though he split the blankets equally with the little man.

As near as he could figure Longarm hadn't slept decently in five or six nights. Maybe more. It had been the desert during the escape, then it had been Rita at the relay station. Then, the previous night, he'd slept with one eye open, afraid one of them would get loose and get away on a horse or find a weapon and ammunition. He felt certain he would sleep this night, but no such thing happened. All night long he would come awake convinced something was wrong. But each time Carl was in his place and the door was still jammed with the chair. He awoke for the last time at dawn, haggard and worn out. He sat up on the bed and looked down. There was Carl Lowe curled up in a ball, sleeping like a puppy. "Hell!" Longarm said disgustedly. He untied the thong from around his ankle and went out to the kitchen to make coffee. Rita was sleeping on top of the table, rolled up from head to foot in blankets. It appeared that everyone had slept except himself.

At around eight in the morning the southbound stage finally pulled in. Good fortune was finally smiling. The guard, who had been a stationkeeper, could work a telegraph key, although he said he was a little rusty. Longarm hustled the man into the stationkeeper's quarters and set him in front of the key. The situation was complicated, but he reduced it to as simple a form as he could. The guard sent the message, and a few minutes later received word back. After that he kept sending and receiving until the situation was made plain. The headquarters for the stage line ordered that the southbound coach go on with the guard driving, while the driver switched to the stage carrying the gold. He was to drive it with all dispatch to company headquarters. He would be met all along the way with fresh teams. It was assumed that Marshal Long would act as guard.

Fresh teams had to be hitched to both coaches. There were no Mexicans to help, but the driver and guard were old hands and soon made short work of the job. Just before the southbound stage was to pull out, Longarm got the driver and guard to help him load the bathtub aboard. He had written a message to the Higginses thanking them for all their help and enclosing a hundred dollars of Riley Hanks's money with the message. He had told Mrs. Higgins it was to be used to buy a new bathtub in case her old one didn't work anymore. The guard took the message and put it in his pocket, but he was still mystified. He said, "How in hell did Mizz Higgins' bathtub get all the way up here? Looks like it has been drug.''

Longarm shook his head wearily. ''They'll tell you all about it. I ain't got the time or the energy.''

They got away, heading north, at a little before eleven that morning. If all went well they should reach Buckeye and the railroad line by five or six that evening.

Longarm took his seat up in the driver's box. He would have much rather sat in the back with his prisoners under the canvas instead of under the sun. He swore to himself that if he got back to Denver alive, he was going to get a room, pull down all the shades, and stay in the dark for a week.

They arrived in the town of Buckeye at a little after five that afternoon. Longarm was forced to spend a little time with the officials of the stage line, but as soon as he could, he headed into town with his prisoners looking for the jail. He shepherded them into a small office and told the sheriff he had two prisoners he wanted put up for the night. But before the sheriff could answer, Rita rounded on him and said, ''You are not going to arrest me! You gave me your word! You sonofabitch, what are you trying to pull?''

He leaned down so he was speaking directly into her face. He said, ''If you'll remember I said that I *personally* didn't care what you and Anson did. And I personally don't. But I'm a deputy U.S. marshal and they don't make deals. You understand the difference? You see what I mean?''

She stamped her foot. ''That's not fair!''

He straightened up. He felt like slapping her violent face. He said, ''Listen, woman, you have been involved in a scheme, up to your neck in it, where seven, eight, nine, maybe more men have been killed and several hundred thousand dollars worth of gold almost got stolen. You are going before a magistrate.''

He turned to the sheriff, who had been looking on with interest. ''Like I say, I need to keep these two on ice for tonight. I ain't had no sleep for a week and I got to get a hotel room and get some.''

The sheriff looked doubtful. ''Wa'l, we ain't set up fer female guests.''

''Hang some blankets. She ain't modest.''

The sheriff scratched his jaw. ''I ain't got but the two cells and one of 'em is occupied.''

''What for?''

''Drunk.''

Longarm reached in his pocket and pulled out a twenty-dollar bill. He said, ''That ought to pay his fine and their keep. I'll give you another one in the morning.''

The sheriff become more interested. ''I'm shore we can he'p you. Allus like to cooperate with the federal law. I'll get these two tucked in and get shut of that drunk.''

When the sheriff came back, Longarm was slumped against one of the desks. The sheriff said, ''All done. Ain't no back door out of this place. Marshal, you look about done in.''

''I am. That westbound train leaves here at one o'clock tomorrow?''

''Yessir.''

Longarm straightened up. ''Then I'll be over at about nine tomorrow morning. You got a magistrate here, don't you?''

''Yessir. Judge Cull.''

''Some officials from the stage line will come along to swear out the complaint. Then I'll be taking the man on that train to Yuma.''

''Hotel is just across the street and down about a block. Can't miss it.''

The next morning Longarm stood looking down at the floor in the sheriff's office. The sheriff said, holding his arms out, ''Marshal, I don't know what happened. I come in the office a little before eight and they was gone. Cell doors was wide open. Reason I didn't come over to the hotel and wake you up was I figured you'd come and got 'em. Changed your mind or something.''

"No," Longarm said, "I didn't change my mind."

"Somebody must have let 'em out. Only thing I can figure."

Longarm sighed. "No, nobody let them out."

"I didn't tell you we didn't have a night man, did I?"

"No, no, you didn't."

Longarm stared back toward the empty cells. He'd had a good supper, a good night's sleep, a shave and a bath, and a fresh change of clothes. He'd thought he was feeling pretty good until he got to the jail. It was his own fault. He must have been out on his feet to have trusted Carl Lowe in a little jail like this one. He wondered if they had gone before he was in bed. He wouldn't have been surprised. He just hoped that Rita didn't get the little man killed before he could get rid of her. But he doubted it.

He said, "When is the next train that would get me up to Denver?"

"Dénver?" The sheriff looked at him questioningly. "I thought you was headed west."

"I was," Longarm said. "I was. Now I want to go to Denver."

The sheriff said, "Well, the train to Phoenix is due in a little over an hour. I reckon you can get a train to Denver from there. Trains run all over out of Phoenix. You figure they are heading for Denver? Your prisoners?"

Longarm turned for the door. He said, "I don't know. But that's where I'm going to start looking." He started toward the hotel to collect his belongings and get down to the train depot. This was one report he'd rather tell his boss, Billy Vail, in person rather than try to write it up.

The sheriff had walked out the door, following him. He said, "Marshal, what makes you think they'll head for Denver?"

Longarm didn't look around. He said, "For one thing,

Denver ain't got no sun nor desert nor mules.''

"What?"

"It's a long story," Longarm said. He shook his head. He reckoned, on balance, he'd done more good than bad. At least he hoped Billy Vail would see it that way.

Watch for

LONGARM AND BRAZOS DEVIL

207th in the bold LONGARM series
from Jove

Coming in March!

Explore the exciting Old West with one of the men who made it wild!